JAN AND THE SEARCH FOR LILYA

THE ITURIA CHRONICLES

J.B. MOONSTAR

BOOK 6

JAN AND THE SEARCH FOR LILYA

THE ITURIA CHRONICLES

J.B. MOONSTAR

Dedication

This book is dedicated to everyone who takes steps to reduce the amount of plastics that are ending up in our oceans and in our wilderness.

Dear Reader,

In my continuing chronicles of the interactions between Ituria's realm and the human world, I will relate the story of a young girl who has recently become part of Ituria's Alliance, determined to help animals who need assistance because of dangers created by humans.

While helping with research on the Chinese Crested Terns, she learns of a group of deer that have been eating food wrappers discarded by humans and are very ill. With the help of her new friend Megan, she agrees to deliver medicine that could bring them back to health; but how will they find the deer needing their help? While on this mission, they discover clues to what may have happened to the missing Nymph Lilya, who disappeared hundreds of years ago.

Can she locate the deer and deliver the medicine in time to save them? And what of the mysterious clues she discovers along the way pointing to Lilya? Jan must decide if she should leave the past hidden or risk releasing new dangers. Only courage will reveal what happened to Lilya. Is she brave enough to search for the truth?

Sincerely,

Knocker,

First Guard to Ituria

TABLE OF CONTENTS

Chapter One

A Meeting
is Requested

Looking over the many tern nests on the rocky cliffs at Site 4, Jan was glad she was able to stay and help the researchers track and report on the latest group of chicks hatching. There had been a lot of changes since Knocker left three weeks ago; the research group hired several local fishermen to act as guards to keep poachers off the island, her father had gone back home, and she was working with Mr. Russell to count the new tern chicks as they hatched.

Able to distinguish between the Chinese Crested Terns and the Greater Crested Terns as the eggs hatched, she recorded the type of tern chick by identifying the parents. The chicks themselves were tiny bundles of tan feathers and mostly hidden from sight. Jan enjoyed taking the time to identify the chick families, as each egg that hatched belonging to the Chinese Crested Tern was one more step further from extinction!

Closing her eyes to enjoy the cooling sea breeze blowing over the cliffs, her mind drifted back to three weeks ago, when she found a small figure leading her to an adventure she would never forget. Reaching into her pocket, she pulled out the little stone statue of a man pointing down and to the left.

This small figure led her and fellow researcher, Knocker, to find Megan, a dragon trapped for 350 years in the cave on Site 3. After Megan was rescued from the cave, Ituria appointed her to take care of the terns they rescued, and Jan had only seen her once since that day. It was a quick trip last week as Megan came to locate and reunite the remaining tern families not transported two weeks earlier. Megan was now on the moon with her charges and Jan understood she must remain there most of the time; however, she hoped Megan was doing well in her new home.

Watching as a small head popped up between the chest and right wing of one of the rare Chinese Crested Terns, she put the figure back in her pocket— another new chick! Tiny, fluffy, tan, and with its mouth wide open, it was ready to be fed. That was the third one today on Site 4. Great news!

While recording the new chick in her journal, another tern landed close to her, looking at her care- fully. It tilted its head to the side, making sure it could see all of her. Something was in its mouth, but what? It didn't look like a fish or other type of food. There was always the danger of terns picking up trash in the water, mistaking it for food. *Should I do anything if the tern tries to feed it to the new chick?*

That didn't seem to be the right question, though, as the tern walked directly toward her and dropped this unknown object in front of her. As Jan watched, the tern pointed to her with its beak, and pointed back to what looked like a small, folded piece of paper. The tern waited cautiously as Jan reached out and carefully picked it up; then she saw the tern nod its head and fly away.

The paper was damp, and Jan unfolded it gently so it would not rip or fall apart. Once opened, she could see it was a group of hand drawn figures and objects. The drawings depicted a cave, a dragon, the moon, and the face of a watch showing 6:00. It also had a drawing of her little figure—*Why would that be there? Who knows about it?* Only Megan, Knocker and Mr. Russell. *What if Megan or Knocker wrote the message?*

Looking at it from a dragon's perspective, she saw one clear interpretation. Since dragons would write in dragon language, she would not be able to read a written message from them. They had drawn items she could understand. Jan knew of the cave where she found Megan, and the moon would mean at night. She read the message as: "Meet me at the cave at six o'clock tonight and bring the figure." *But why the figure?*

Jan pulled out the figure once more, carefully examining it from head to toe. The back had a circle on it, and there was something carved inside. It was hard to make out what may have been carved in the black stone, though. Taking a blank piece of paper from her notebook, she placed it on top of the circle, then rubbed her pencil lead back and forth lightly to see if she could make a copy of what was carved on the figure. *There is something there!*

While only about an inch across, the circle contained what looked like a flower in the middle, surrounded by a long lizard-like, fire-breathing dragon circling around the outside of the flower. *A dragon?*

Why would a small carved figure from 350 years ago have a circle on its shirt with a dragon? Jan jumped up and headed back to camp; she wanted to look this up on her computer before the meeting tonight. *There must be a reason!*

Chapter Two

ANOTHER FIGURE

Running quickly up the path, Jan wanted to make sure she was on time. It was almost six o'clock as she got to the top of the cliff on Site 3. There were not as many terns here as on the other sites, as some of the eggs had been stolen by poachers. Later rescued by Knocker and Megan, both the parents and eggs were transported to Ituria's Islands in the caverns of the moon and were now under the watchful care of Megan.

Jan made it to the front of the cave just as her watch clicked to six. Looking up to the moon, she wondered what would happen next. Suddenly, blue light flashed from the sky, and Megan appeared at the cave in front of Jan in her human form. Megan's ruby-red dress and dark grey hair reminded Jan of the shiny ruby scales and large grey wings of Megan's dragon form.

"I am so glad to see you!" exclaimed Jan excitedly as she ran over to Megan; however, a little concern crept into her voice as she continued, "Is everything okay? Are you okay?"

"Hi, Jan." Megan replied calmly. "So good to see you again. Yes, I am fine." Megan smiled and bowed gracefully as dragons do when they greet someone. Jan bowed back to greet her dragon friend.

"I need your assistance on a couple of things," she added. "Ituria said it would be okay if I came back to Earth if you accompanied me on my journey. As you know, I'm still very new to interacting with humans."

"I'll be glad to help, of course. You know that. What happened? What do you need?" Jan asked, worried about the reason for Megan's return.

"There are two things I need to accomplish," Megan started, talking quickly to explain her quest. "The first thing we need to do is to save several deer that are sick; I have obtained medicine to help them get well. The terns I met last week told me of a group of deer that are fed by humans and may have also been eating food coverings discarded by humans on the ground. We need to get to them very soon to provide some medicine to help them."

Megan paused for a moment and looked anxiously at Jan. Closing her eyes, she took a deep breath and then opened them again. "The second is a personal assignment," she said hesitantly. "I need your help to see if we can find Lilya."

Jan's eyes widened as she looked back at Megan, very confused at this request.

"But how can you find Lilya? Do you have any idea where she may be?" Jan's mind started racing as she remembered the Nymph Lilya left Megan chained to a wall in a cave about 350 years ago; Jan and Knocker had freed Megan only three weeks ago. *How can they trace something that happened so long ago?*

Carefully pulling a small figure out of her satchel, Megan held it up and showed it to Jan. Jan couldn't believe her eyes—*another figure*! It was a carved figure of a horse, its carving style and material matched Jan's figure. *They must be connected!*

"This figure was in the root ball of the tree that you and Knocker took from the cave. We were planting it when this fell out. Look, it has markings on it; although I'm not sure what they mean." Holding up the horse, she pointed to a carved blanket draped over the small stone horse, covering its back. Carved into the blanket were six small circles, each only about a half-inch wide.

Looking closely, Jan could see something carved into the circles but couldn't make out what was there. Pulling out a sheet of paper and placing it on the horse's back, she rubbed a pencil over the top as she did before. Each of the circles had a carved flower inside. The flowers looked like the same type of flower but drawn differently—and she realized it was the same flower that she found in the circle drawing on the back of her figure!

"Megan, this could be a clue!" Jan exclaimed. "When I got your message, I looked at my figure and

I found a circle on the back." Pulling her figure out, she excitedly showed Megan the figure's back and the circle, along with the paper and pencil shading from earlier today. Holding the two pieces of paper together, she exclaimed, "My circle contained a flower just like yours, but mine also has a dragon circling outside the flower."

"I looked up the circle on my figure when I got your note and found that many years ago people used family crests on their clothes and houses to identify themselves to others. Each crest was different, although many had the same themes or subject matter. Since our circles are similar, this could be a clue to finding Lilya, but I'm not sure what it means yet or how it can help us."

"Well, once we complete our first mission, maybe we can spend a little time to find out if it holds any clues to where Lilya is ... and why she left me!" Megan's voice was full of emotion now, as the memory of being chained to the cave wall for hundreds of years was still fresh in her mind.

"I will be glad to help you, whatever you want to do. You know that." Jan said supportively, reaching out and gently touching Megan's arm to calm her. Attempting to draw Megan's attention away from the memories of the cave, she continued quietly, "But first we need to get to the deer, right? How did you learn about them?"

Megan nodded, refocused her thoughts, and replied, "A tern said she heard about them from other terns who live over the mountains. She gave me instructions of how to get there." Megan again reached into her satchel and pulled out a piece of paper with some drawings on it.

"Here is where the cave is—where we are now," Megan continued, pointing to her map. "Flying east over this set of mountains and almost to the sea on the other side, there is a human community that feeds a whole herd of deer. Right about here," Megan said as she pointed to a spot on the map that had been circled. "This is where we need to go first. One of the residents of Ituria's Island has created a medicine to dissolve plastic into liquid and small pellets, allowing the animal to throw them up without damaging their body. Simon originally created it for sea turtles; however, he said it should work on deer also."

Once again opening her satchel, Megan pulled out and held up a small jar containing about thirty small pills. "Let's proceed with the deer mission first. That is our top priority." As she put the map and pills back, she added, "Then we can look further into the mystery of the circles!"

Chapter Three

CALL FOR HELP

After a brief discussion with Mr. Russell, the research leader and a good friend of Ituria's, Jan and Megan headed back to Site 4. Since Megan would have to fly to the deer's location, it was better that they travel at night, and it was almost dark now. Questions could arise if a dragon were spotted flying around during the day. Megan's night vision was almost as good as her day vision, especially tonight where the moonlight allowed her to see for miles.

As they walked, Megan explained more about what the terns had told her.

"There is a place where humans have designated that the deer shall not be harmed, so many deer have decided to stay in the area. The humans like to interact with the deer, so the humans started feeding them. The deer, not knowing what human food is edible and not edible, have started eating the wrappers thrown on the ground as the humans leave."

"I met Simon," she continued, "who is the creator of the pills I brought. He has been treating sick sea creatures for a long time; those that eat something called plastic thinking it may be food. They ingest so much plastic that their stomachs are stuffed, and they cannot absorb any nutrition from what little real food they do eat. Although the deer are not sea creatures, it sounds like they have the same illness according to Simon, so I am to find them and provide the medicine to help them get better."

"That sounds like a good solution for now," Jan replied. "Is there any way to keep the deer from eating the discarded wrappers?"

"Not at this point," Megan answered, shaking her head, "other than to tell them not to eat anything off the ground put there by humans. Ituria and I discussed that issue, and until the humans stop throwing trash on the ground that smells like food, it will be hard for the deer to know what is safe to eat."

Reaching into her pocket, Megan took out a small flat stone and handed it to Jan. "Ituria said that you should keep this, so that you can communicate with the deer when we meet them. They will understand me, but they will not understand human speak."

Nodding with understanding, Jan put the translation stone in her pocket. "I remember how important this is, and I will keep it safe and return it to you once we get back to the research site."

Reaching Site 4, it was time to start their journey.

"Okay, Megan, if you will allow, once you have transformed, I'll ride on your back," Jan said respectfully, knowing one doesn't just jump on the back of a large dragon without permission.

Megan nodded and agreed. "Yes, that would be the best way to travel. Let me make sure that we will not be seen, and then we can be on our way."

Jan stood back and watched as Megan looked over the cliff on Site 4, making sure there would be no one to see her transform into her dragon form. Then she closed her eyes for just a moment and turned into a fantastically large, ruby-scaled dragon, standing twice as tall as Jan and almost 20 feet long. Jan had forgotten just how beautiful she was in her dragon form, her ruby scales shimmering in the setting sun.

"That always amazes me, and you are so beautiful!" Jan exclaimed.

"Thank you for your kind words, Jan," Megan replied. "I am just getting used to these transformations. As Knocker explained, I must wait a week between using the magic potion that gives me the ability to transform into a human. That's why I had to wait a week before I could return to meet with you, and why we must get to the deer as soon as possible."

Jan walked over and climbed onto Megan's back, settling in between her left wing and the row of dark grey spikes that lined her back from her neck to her tail. Jan would need to hold on very tight, as she had never ridden on a dragon before.

Once she felt secure, Jan called to Megan. "I'm ready to go!"

One more quick look around and Megan effortlessly launched herself into the sky, flying almost straight up until she was high enough to be hidden in the clouds. Jan held on even tighter and closed her eyes.

Flapping her large, grey wings, Megan easily flew over the mountaintops, and after about an hour, they reached the spot on the map where she was to land to find the deer. Still high in the sky, Megan searched for an isolated area to land, peering into the darkness below them.

"Jan, I'll land over there near the forest, and then we can walk in," Megan called back. "I don't want to be spotted getting too close to the humans' buildings."

"That sounds like a good idea!" Jan called back as she cautiously opened her eyes and looked around at the surrounding clouds, glad they were finally heading back to solid ground.

"Hold on!" Megan shouted back to Jan. "We are going down quickly, so we won't be seen!"

Jan was already holding on very tightly, as flying in the open air hundreds of feet above the ground at night was thrilling, but also scary. "I'm holding on!" she called back.

As Megan made a nosedive for a small clearing in the forest, Jan held on even tighter, closed her eyes, and pressed her head on the back of Megan's neck, hoping they would land without crashing.

Chapter Four

FINDING THE DEER

Once she was close to the ground, Megan slowed and lightly touched down. She turned her neck and looked at Jan, crouching against her, clenching Megan's spikes with her eyes tightly shut. "Jan, we've landed," she called back quietly, so as not to scare her further.

Jan opened her eyes and looked up, quite surprised. She was still waiting for the big jolt she was expecting when they crashed to the ground. Glad they were back on land, she exclaimed, "Thank you, Megan, that was so amazing!"

"I haven't been able to fly like that in forever!" The exhilaration from her flight over the mountains reflected in her voice. "I haven't done that since I was a tiny dragon, and I was never allowed to fly so high!"

Megan's excitement at flying matched Jan's excitement at being able to stand on solid ground. "I am so glad you enjoyed that, Megan," Jan replied. "I'm glad to be back on the ground for now. It is astounding how fast and silently you can fly through the air. I'm so impressed!"

"It was fun! Now, let's see if we can find the sick deer," Megan said. "But first, I'll need to transform." Megan closed her eyes to concentrate. This time it took a little longer for her to transform. It was exciting being able to fly again, making it harder for Megan to convince herself to become calm and transform into a tiny, wingless human. After a few moments, she was able to accomplish the transformation and smiled at Jan with her human face. "I don't know how you live in this form—so small!"

"I agree I am much smaller than a dragon," Jan replied. "But it's all I've ever been, so I'm used to it." She smiled back and looked around to see where they had ended up.

The field where they landed was next to a small area of thick forest. However, while there were many tall trees creating a large canopy for the forest creatures, there were only a few spots that were not cleared near the ground. Possibly, since the deer lived here without fear of being hunted, they kept the underbrush cleared out. As Jan and Megan walked through the forest, they noticed various groups of deer sitting together, and headed towards one of the larger groups.

"Greetings from Ituria!" Megan called out to them as she approached the group. "I am Megan. Ituria has asked me to assist with some deer who have fallen ill. Can you help me find them?"

A large buck quickly stood up to guard his family. "How can you talk to us, human Megan?" The buck sniffed the air several times, looked closely at Megan, and then continued, a little confused. "Are you human? I smell human and something else." Then his voice changed quickly to a challenge. "Please explain yourself before coming any closer to my family." Moving rapidly, the buck positioned himself between Megan and the other deer in his group, who were just waking up because of the commotion.

"I am not human, but a dragon in human form. It is safer to travel this way on Earth. I bring you greetings from Ituria." Megan then bowed to the buck to show her respect. She turned to Jan and continued, "This is my human friend, Jan, who is here to help me find and care for some deer who we were told were very sick."

"Where did you come from?" he answered back, challenging them to explain why they were in the deer's sleeping grounds. "This area is supposed to be blocked from humans at night; that's why we rest here." The buck's defensive tone revealed that he didn't really trust these humans yet.

"Please know that we mean you and your family no harm," Megan said, then paused. She was not quite sure what she could say to make the deer understand. *Maybe if I explained how I learned of the sick deer?*

"I was talking to a tern named Sarah about a week ago, and she talked with a deer named Bonnie from this area. Bonnie relayed that there were several deer that were very sick and asked that if Sarah saw Ituria, to ask him to send help. Ituria has sent us to help them. Do you know a deer named Bonnie?"

Turning to the group of deer sitting behind him, and looking at one near the front, he asked, "Bonnie, does that sound correct? Did you talk to a tern named Sarah?"

"Yes, John," she replied as she stood and walked over the group. "I talked with Sarah and her mate, Michael. At the time, I was trying to help the sick deer to eat and drink but wasn't having much luck. I mentioned it to Sarah, and she said she would check to see if anything could be done. Sarah indicated that she would be going to Ituria's Island soon and they might have a cure."

Turning to Megan and Jan, Bonnie continued, "Since you are here and know of Sarah, perhaps you can tell us what solutions you have brought. There are ten deer being treated now, and sadly another passed away several days ago. The humans found him and removed him from the forest."

"Greetings, Bonnie," Megan said as she bowed to her. "On behalf of Ituria, I have been provided with medicine created by a healer." As she took the jar of pills out of her satchel and showed them to Bonnie, she continued, "These pills were developed by Simon to help dissolve plastic waste that may have been left by humans and eaten by the deer."

"Well, I trust Ituria, so if he sent you, I trust you also." Bonnie bowed her head in greeting to Megan, and then quickly continued. "We should go visit the deer as soon as possible to get them the medicine. Follow me!" Bonnie suddenly turned and started running into one the few stands of deep brush remaining in the forest.

It took only a few minutes before they emerged into an opening where numerous deer were laying on the ground, and other deer were talking to them or bringing them water. Those that were sick were barely moving; however, all turned and looked at Bonnie as she led Megan and Jan into the clearing.

"Bonnie, what are you doing?" One of the helper deer exclaimed in fear. "There are humans following you; why have you led them here?"

"This is Megan, who has been sent by Ituria to help you get better," Bonnie replied. Turning to Megan, she continued with urgency, "Megan, please administer the medicine now, as some of these deer have little time left."

Chapter Five

TIME FOR MEDICINE

Megan nodded and motioned for Jan to follow her. Walking into the middle of the clearing and looking around at the sick deer, she explained what would be happening.

"Ituria has discussed your conditions with a healer, Simon, who was determined that you may be suffering from the same illness as the sea turtles Simon treats. Please confirm the following fits your actions and symptoms, so we can determine if the medicine will work for you."

Looking around at the deer, she continued, "This medicine is created to dissolve the wrappers that contained food smells that you may have eaten. If your stomach feels full and you are unable to eat, this pill should help you." The deer laying on the were nodding their heads as best they could in their current condition, agreeing that the symptoms were the same.

"However," Megan continued with a little worry in her voice, "be aware that to cure you, we need to get the human trash out of your stomachs, so Simon said you will find yourself spitting out the dissolved wrappers that have been blocking your system."

Megan walked around as she explained to make sure they understood what would be happening. "This will take several hours, but Simon has created a pill that will render the plastic into small pellets so it will cause no permanent damage to your stomach. You will need to take this with some water and need to continue drinking water until all the trash has been thrown up and your stomach feels empty. Are there any questions before we get started?"

The deer shook their heads. Their eyes were opened wide, and a glimmer of hope appeared on their faces, they were ready to try anything that would help them feel better.

"Bonnie," Megan continued. "Can you please assign a deer to help each of the sick ones, to make sure they have access to water for the next several hours?"

"Jan, please come with me to help administer the pills, it may take both of us to give the pills and follow up with the water," Megan said. Jan saw a bucket that had some water in it; she picked it up and walked over to Megan.

"Ready to start whenever you are, Megan!" Jan replied.

"How can she understand you?" asked Bonnie with surprise. First looking at Megan, then at Jan, she said, "I thought you were a dragon, Megan. How is this possible? Humans never understand us when we talk to them."

"Yes, I can understand you," Jan replied to Bonnie. "Ituria has provided me with one of his translation stones, which allows me to understand you and Megan. Please allow me to be included in your plans to save the deer. I am more than happy to help!"

"Yes, Jan, of course!" Bonnie answered. "I'm so glad that you can understand me. Your assistance will be invaluable when helping the deer to drink water."

"Let's get started. The sooner they get the medicine, the sooner they will feel better," Jan said and followed Megan as she walked toward the first deer.

"Greetings. I am Megan. I want to share this medicine to make you feel better," Megan said as she bowed to the deer.

Very slowly, the deer responded, "Greetings, Megan; I am Sasha. Thank you for your help." She tried to lift her head off the ground as she replied but could not raise her head more than a few inches.

"Here, let me help you," Jan said softly as she knelt beside Sasha and lifted the deer's head into a more upright position. This allowed Megan to place a pill in her mouth and for her to take a small drink of water. "Hopefully, you will be better soon!" Jan tried to sound cheerful; however, the deer was very weak. She wondered if they had gotten to her in time.

Bonnie followed behind Megan and Jan, assigning a helper deer to stay with each of the sick deer as they received the medicine. Within twenty minutes, all had received the medicine. Now, they could only wait to see if it would help.

It did not take too long before the medicine started working, and the deer started throwing up the dissolved plastic. It came out in the form of small pellets of plastic mixed in with saliva that protected their throat and stomach as they threw up.

"Bonnie!" Megan called out. "Please make sure that all the deer have someone to give them water. We must keep them hydrated!"

Megan turned to Jan and added, "Jan, because you and I are able to hold the water buckets and assist them to drink, we will need to visit each one to help make sure they get enough water. This medicine will dehydrate them if they throw up numerous times."

"Understood," Jan agreed. "I'll handle this side, and I'll let you handle that side. That way we can each keep track of five of them, and we won't miss anyone."

"I agree!" Megan said as she went to one of them to assist.

Bonnie and the helper deer, along with Megan and Jan, spent most of the night making sure each of the sick deer took a drink of water as often as possible as they purged the harmful plastic from their stomachs. As dawn approached, most the deer were quietly sleeping.

Bonnie and Megan went off to gather some soft food to feed them when they woke. Simon had instructed Megan to make sure to start feeding them as soon as they stopped throwing up; their bodies were starving because the plastic blocked their stomach from digesting food.

Jan looked at the piles of plastic pellets near each of them. It was unbelievable to her that they each had so much of this trash in their stomach. Each pile was about the size of a gallon milk container.

There must be a way to stop this, but what can be done? She could not come up with a solution because as long as people carelessly threw food wrappers on the ground that smelled like the treats they feed the deer; the deer would end up eating the discarded wrappers also.

As Megan and Bonnie came back with some food, Megan motioned for Jan to come over.

"Jan," she said quietly, "Bonnie has agreed to watch over the deer for a few hours, since they are sleeping now. She will give each a little food and water as they wake up, and we'll be back soon to help." In an excited whisper, she continued, "I just saw something that I need to show you."

Chapter Six

CIRCLES

"What is it, Megan?" Jan whispered as they got out of hearing range of the deer.

"As Bonnie and I were walking along the edge of the deer conservation area to gather food, there were houses on the other side of the fence. Many of these houses have a circle above the entrance!" Megan's voice revealed her excitement as she stopped and pointed to the houses. "And look at the circles! Many of them have a flower in the circle! Do you still have the paper showing the flower designs?"

"Yes, I do!" Jan exclaimed, reaching into her backpack to get the papers. "Here is the one from the horse blanket you found." Jan pointed to the circles. "There are six different circles, but each is very similar. They all look like the same flower."

After handing Megan the paper, Jan pulled out the circle from the statue she had found. "And the flower on this is very similar to those you have. The only difference is the dragon circling around the flower!"

The two held their papers together, comparing the drawings inside the circles. Would they be able to match them to the circles on the houses?

Sunrise was half an hour ago, so the people were starting to walk along the streets.

"Megan," whispered Jan. "We need to try to blend in, act like we are visitors—tourists—just enjoying the scenery, okay?"

"What should I do?" Megan asked with a puzzled look on her face. "I don't know what you mean." Being trapped in a cave for 350 years didn't allow her to develop the ability to blend in with humans. "Tell me what I should be doing, okay?"

"Yes, of course," Jan said. "Just walk slowly and look at the houses. Look at all of the house and not just the circles." Jan stopped walking and pointed to a pretty tree in front of one of the houses. Softly, she said to Megan, "You just look and nod your head. You can't let people hear your dragon voice, okay?" Then in a voice that was a little louder than necessary, Jan exclaimed, "Look how pretty that tree is, the flowers are beautiful!"

Megan nodded and smiled as she pointed at the flowers blooming on the tree.

Jan nodded and continued walking down the street. As they walked, they looked carefully at each circle, then Jan made remarks about something else about the houses—how elegant the roof was shaped, the beautiful fountain, anything but the circles they were tracking.

Some of the houses in this area looked very old, while others were much newer. Over the hundreds of years of everyday living, the use of the houses and land surrounding them must have changed.

"It looks like some of the houses are very old, and possibly had gardens between them; then as the city grew, the gardens were replaced by newer houses," Jan remarked loudly as she pointed at the different architecture of the various houses. Then she continued quietly to Megan, "Do you see only the older houses have the circles?"

"Yes, I see!" Megan replied softly, nodding her head in agreement.

"You can tell by the difference in the roofs," Jan continued, "and how the windows are set."

As they walked down the street, Jan pointed to various houses, calling out differences in the architecture and whether there were small gardens still visible. Quietly, she was checking each of the circles that were part of the older houses, noting to herself that many had a variation of the flowers that she and Megan found on the horse statue's blanket.

"Megan," she called out as she pointed to one of the older houses. "Look at that roof. How old do you think that house is?"

Megan turned to look at what Jan was pointing to and saw an older house with a circle displayed on the front. It was across the street, so they crossed to get a closer look.

Megan nodded her head and talked softly to Jan, "I see it! The circle here almost matches the one on your figure's back!"

"It has to be hundreds of years old!" Jan replied louder so all could hear. Then whispering excitedly to Megan, she added, "The only difference is the crescent moon. I wonder if this is the place!"

"What should we do now? Can we ask the owner what it means?" Megan wondered, trying to figure out their next step. "Maybe they can help us!"

"We can try, but we will need to be very careful, Megan. Remember, only you will be able to understand what they are saying, I cannot. The translation stone does not translate human languages. I learned that when you were yelling at the poachers last time. I could not understand them, even though you could." Jan was trying to determine how to proceed.

"Okay, I understand," Megan replied. "I will try and repeat what they say, so you will know what is going on." Looking back at the house, Megan took a quick breath and grabbed Jan's arm. "Jan, there is someone looking at us from the window. Now what?"

Chapter Seven

CREST EXPLAINED

"Okay, Megan, remain calm," Jan whispered. "That is your most important job—you must remain calm at all times."

Megan nodded slowly. "But what should we do? Look, they are coming out of the door now!"

Jan looked over at the front door of the house as a man walked outside, heading their way. "Megan, when he is within ten feet you can talk to him," Jan whispered. "Tell him you think his house is beautiful and wondered what the circle on top near the roof means."

Both watched silently as an older man walked toward them. As soon as he was within ten feet, Megan introduced herself.

"Greetings. I am Megan. Pleased to make your acquaintance," Megan said, then bowed as dragons do.

The older man smiled when he saw her bow. He spoke to Megan and bowed back.

"We were admiring your home; it is very historic and well kept. How old is it?" Megan asked.

Megan nodded as the man was explaining some-thing, then she nodded to Jan.

Jan was listening but could only understand Megan's side.

"So, your house is over 500 years old? Very impressive. Does that circle on the front have a spe-cial meaning, or is it a beautiful decoration?"

The man stood up straight, obviously proud of the crest Megan had mentioned, then spent a few minutes explaining what the crest was for as he pointed to it.

"Now I see! The first owner was a samurai who called him-self the dragon warrior. That is where the dragon comes from." Megan wanted to make sure Jan knew the story. "And the flower, that's a cherry blossom from the beautiful trees locally. But why is there the moon? I don't quite understand that part," Megan asked.

The man continued with his story, smiling and gesturing, obviously proud of his family history, and this time Megan's eyes widened as he explained why the moon appeared.

"You first only had the dragon and flower on the family crest, but your ancestors trapped a moon god-dess to raise your bonsai plant? And so, your family added the moon to your crest. How did that happen?"

The man added a few more sentences to his story, then asked a question of Megan.

"Of course, we would love to see your family bonsai tree. Thank you for your kind offer!" Megan's excitement was evident in her voice, and Jan gently slipped her hand into Megan's, trying to calm her down.

"Yes, please allow me to introduce my friend Jan. She does not speak your language, but I am sure she would also be very glad to view your family bonsai garden." Megan turned and pointed to Jan as she spoke, and Jan bowed to him. The man bowed back and smiled at Jan. The man stood tall, and his eyes shined as he continued his story, and Jan could tell he was very proud of his bonsai tree.

As the man started to walk back to the door, he motioned for them to follow. Jan whispered to Megan. "Two things—take off your shoes on the porch and bow before you go in the door—that is the custom here."

"Thanks," Megan whispered back and followed Jan's instructions. As they got to the door, the man took off his sandals and left them just inside the house, and Megan and Jan did the same, bowing as they went through the door.

The house owner seemed pleased by these actions, said something to Megan, and motioned for them to follow him as he headed for a room to the right of the entrance.

"You have a magical bonsai?" Megan said in response to the man's words. "What do you mean by that?"

Motioning for them to follow him, the man continued, quickly speaking as he was excited to share his family's story to these two visitors. After letting him finish his story, Megan repeated it so Jan could understand.

"The tree is only supposed to live for fifty years, and it has lived for over three hundred and fifty years? That is amazing! How did you do that?" Megan's question caused the man to look at her for a moment, his eyes narrowing, and his smile disappeared.

He started answering her question—or possibly changed the subject of the conversation. Jan was not sure where the conversation was leading and watched both Megan and the man closely. His voice got quieter as he explained something to Megan, then started using hand motions and seemed to be getting upset, and his voice got louder again. This time it wasn't a proud or boastful tone, but almost menacing. Megan was staring at him intently, following each word he spoke.

"I understand," Megan replied softly, nodding her head. "Keeping the tree healthy is a family secret, and you do not have to reveal your secret." That seemed to calm him down again, and he smiled and nodded back.

Jan looked at Megan, her eyes wide and a little panicked; for the first time, she wondered if trying to solve this mystery was such a good idea. They were now in the house of someone they didn't know who had a family secret he didn't want to share. Where was this going to lead?

Chapter Eight

TREE OF LEGEND

Turning to the right, the man led them down a narrow hallway. As they walked, Jan could hear little chirping sounds, like little birds. *But the noise is coming from the floor.* Megan must have heard it too, and asked, "What are the chirping sounds? Do you have birds in the house?"

This started the man on a new story; his eyes lit up as he described what the sounds were and was showing Megan that the chirping happened every time he stepped on one of the floorboards. Jan couldn't understand this. *Why would you want your floors to squeak?*

Megan, on the other hand, was very interested, nodding and smiling. "I see!" she said once he was done. "The Samurai who built the house, your ancestor, put in what were called nightingale floors, to protect them from intruders. Any intruders would be heard walking on the floors and would not be able to sneak up on the Samurai master. How clever!"

They turned to the right and went through a small door into what appeared to be a small outdoor garden. Jan looked up and saw large beams stretching from one side of the garden to the other covering the entire garden area. Covering the beams was a large rope net; it would allow the sunlight and rain to get in, but no one could get out. And rather than have dirt and plants, the garden was paved in stone with one large pot in the middle holding a bonsai tree. Jan tried to get Megan's attention. *There is something wrong here. Why is there a net over the beams, and why is the garden paved?*

But Megan was staring in the direction of the bonsai tree located in the center of the garden. It was a beautiful bonsai tree—the trunk was very thick, and the branches had been meticulously trimmed to keep it to a height of only about four feet. It was in a large pot about three feet high and four feet wide at the top, so the pot and tree were an awesome sight, together standing about seven feet tall.

And near the bottom of the bonsai pot, almost unnoticed because of the great size and beauty of the bonsai, was a small apple tree in a pot beside it.

Jan gasped as she saw it; it looked exactly like the apple tree that Megan had been trapped guarding in the cave! There were small green apples hanging off the delicate branches, not yet ready to eat.

Her mind was drawn away from the apple tree as the man started rapidly talking while pointing to the bonsai tree and showing how he carefully trimmed the branches. He wanted to make sure Megan knew how much care had been taken to keep this tree alive. Jan looked at the man who was so proud of his bonsai tree as he continued talking to Megan, but Megan could only stare at the apple tree.

Walking over next to Megan, Jan touched Megan's arm and whispered, "You must be calm, remember."

Whispering back, Megan replied, "I am trying. Can you see the apple tree? Lilya was here."

Neither noticed the man had stopped talking and was listening to them closely. He could not understand what Jan said, however, when Megan whispered the word Lilya, his reaction was immediate.

He started yelling at them both. His face turned red, and he went to stand in front of the trees and was shaking his arms at them, then he ran toward the door. As his rant continued, he opened the door and swung his left arm toward the door and his finger pointed out—he wanted them to leave now!

Talking loudly over the continued yelling, Megan replied, "Why are you so mad? Are you not proud of your tree?" After pausing for a moment, she quietly added, "Do you know who Lilya was? Was she here?" Megan was talking slowly—deliberately choosing her words—she was trying to retain control of her emotions. This man knew something about Lilya, and Megan had to remain calm enough to find out what he knew.

This question made the man stop yelling, but he still pointed to the door, gesturing with his arms that they must leave. He would say no more; he had revealed too much already.

"Was Lilya here?" Megan repeated, her voice stronger and showing she had no intention of leaving without an answer.

"I still am," said a small voice as Lilya appeared next to the trees.

Chapter Nine

TRAPPED

Megan glared at the man and shouted angrily. "What have you done?!"

His eyes widened and his jaw dropped as he realized the secret to keeping the bonsai alive for hundreds of years had been revealed. Shouting one more time at them all, he immediately ran out of the room and slammed the door behind him. A jingle of keys could be heard from the other side of the door, then a clunk as the door was locked from the outside. *We're trapped!*

However, to Jan, there was a more immediate concern as Megan stared at Lilya, unable to speak further, her fists clenched in anger. Jan could see in Megan's face that her emotions were fighting within her. Her eyes narrowed and her eyebrows were furrowed; her lips were closed tightly. She was trying to keep herself from releasing her anger at being trapped for so many years. Megan was furious with Lilya for leaving her in the cave, yet she had just learned that Lilya was trapped here, so maybe it wasn't that Lilya forgot about her; what if Lilya was also trapped? Would that change the focus of her rage?

Stepping between Lilya and Megan, Jan looked directly at Megan and tried to block her view of Lilya. "Please," she said as calmly as she could, "don't do anything until we know what happened, please!"

But it was Lilya who spoke next. "Who are you and how do you know who I am?"

Jan quickly turned and looked at Lilya. *She can understand me, but how?*

"Can you understand me? I can understand you," Jan blurted out. "I'm not sure why, but I can understand you."

"Yes, I can understand you—but I shouldn't be able to," Lilya replied, equally perplexed.

"Jan, the stone, remember? That's how you understand me, too." Megan spoke quietly, still trying to remain calm. "Lilya, how did you come to be here?"

Jan relaxed a little. *At least she is giving Lilya a chance to explain!*

"I have been trapped here for hundreds of years." Lilya's voice was soft and sad. "When I came to this area, I was befriended by a powerful samurai warrior. He pretended to like me once he realized I could help his plants grow. He promised to protect me and had his workers build me a home in a cave to live. However, just before I was to move to the cave, he trapped me here—*with this bonsai tree*—and told me if it ever died that he would kill me!" Lilya's voice broke and she started crying. Continuing through her tears, she explained, "The samurai and his descendants have kept me trapped here, with no way to escape, each vowing that if this tree dies, so do I." Lilya put her head in her hands and continued crying softly.

Wanting to know more before she said anything else, Megan asked, "Do you remember Megan?"

"Yes, I do!" Lilya said as she looked up, a little surprised by the question. "I think of her every day. It breaks my heart! She does not know why I didn't come back. If you free me, we need to save her!" Lilya was frantic now. Looking desperately at Megan and Jan through tear-filled eyes, she continued. "But we are trapped, don't you see! There is no way out of this garden for me … or for you." Stopping for a moment, she added, "How do you know about Megan?"

"Lilya…" Megan started, then sighed, her eyes filled with tears. "I am here to find you." Then she stopped talking, too overcome by emotion to continue.

Seeing that Megan needed time to get control over her feelings, Jan wanted to help Lilya understand what had happened but wasn't sure how much to reveal. "Megan, do you want me to explain?"

Megan raised her palm to Jan and shook her head. "No, I will explain. It will make more sense if I do. Just give me a moment." Megan took another deep breath to regain her composure.

"Megan?" Lilya asked. "Are you also called Megan? Do you know of my Megan? How?"

"I *am* your Megan," she replied. "Your story and mine are intertwined. I was trapped for hundreds of years in the cave where you left me, and Jan found me. Now," she paused to take another deep breath, "I have found you."

"Megan? How can you be my Megan?" Lilya asked. "My Megan is a dragon."

"When Jan and Knocker rescued me, they used a magic potion that allowed me to transform to a human, so I could escape the cave. I have used that potion to allow me to return to Earth in human form." Her voice was still tense, very stilted and without emotion, as she worked hard to hold back her true feelings.

"Megan ... my Megan?" Lilya exclaimed. "I am so sorry! I did plan on coming back. You must believe me! Not one day goes by that I don't think of you, knowing that you are trapped. I am so sorry!" Tears started flowing from Lilya's eyes again as she realized Megan had been freed. "Thank you, Jan, for saving my Megan," she said in a broken voice. "You are no longer trapped in the cave. That was my biggest regret—that I could not reach you. Please forgive me, Megan. I beg of you! I would not have left you there alone so long if I could have done anything to get to you."

"I understand, Lilya," Megan replied quietly, regaining her self-control. "We can discuss why you put me in the cave to begin with later, but that is not our first concern. First, we must get away from here, and there does not appear a way to leave at this time."

Lilya nodded, pulling her mind back to the current situation. "I agree, but the two trees here are chained to the ground." She pointed to the chains binding the potted trees, then continued. "Being a

Forest Nymph, I must be always in contact with a plant, so I cannot leave this prison. However, please know I will do whatever I can to make sure both of you are able to escape."

Noises from outside the door warned many people were gathering outside. The nightingale floors were chirping as footsteps could be heard running up and down the hallway.

Mumbling of many voices could be heard outside the door, then one shouted loudly and footsteps were heard running away.

"We must hurry!" Megan said. "They are going to get their dragon. We must be gone before they get back!"

Chapter Ten

MAKING THEIR ESCAPE

"**O**kay," Megan continued. "We must break out of here before the dragon arrives, and Lilya, we are not leaving you here." There was no questioning the determination in Megan's voice.

"But I can't leave!" Lilya argued. "I am just as chained to the floor as these trees, for if I go away from them even for a few minutes, I will die! You must leave without me!"

"No, that is not an option," Megan replied. She would not be leaving Lilya behind.

"Megan," Jan said, "remember how Knocker was able to break your chains, even in human form? See if you can do that. If so, then Lilya can take the apple tree with her. It is small enough for her to carry."

"Good idea, Jan," Megan answered as she walked over to the thick chains looped through the pots and held by large locks onto the pavement below. Lifting a portion of the chain to the apple tree off the ground, she stomped on it. The chain links bent and did not break at first, but a few more stomps and the chain link broke in two, freeing the apple tree from the floor.

"How can you do that?" Lilya asked in disbelief. "How can you break metal like that?"

"Over the past 350 years, I have grown into a rather large dragon," Megan responded calmly. "Knocker showed me that even if I am in this tiny human form, I still have the strength of a full-grown dragon. That's how I am able to break metal." Megan's voice softened as she added, "You will be surprised at how much I have changed, Lilya. I am no longer a baby dragon."

Walking around the garden, Megan surveyed the situation. "We can't go out through the door. It's blocked," Megan said. "They have put furniture in front of it so we cannot open it to get through, even if I am able to break the lock. There are also men waiting on the other side, and I can't risk you two being injured. What are our other options?"

"I remember that this garden is in the front part of the house— possibly we can break through the front wall and get out?" Jan looked at all the walls and thought back to the steps and turns they had taken to get to this room. She pointed to the one she determined to be the front wall based on the layout of the portion of the house they walked through. "This wall will lead us to the street. What do you think, Megan? Can you burn through the wall to get us out?"

"I can try. That would require that I turn back into a dragon, though, and I'm not sure there is enough room here to do that." Looking up, Megan continued, "The other option would be to burn the beams and go out through the roof. Both options require I turn into a dragon."

"Agreed," Jan replied. "Let's see how far Lilya and I can get from you. Lilya, you will need to hold onto your tree, okay?" Jan reached down and picked up the apple tree and pot, detaching it from the broken chain. It was much smaller than the bonsai tree, with the pot being about a foot tall with the apple tree being a few feet tall above it.

Lilya was able to hold it in her left hand, hugging the pot with the small tree trunk resting on her shoulder. "This will work!" she exclaimed excitedly as she walked around the garden on the pavement. "I can finally leave this place!"

"Great! First step done," replied Jan. "Second step, Megan has to transform. Let's get over to this corner and give her as much room as possible." She and Lilya moved over to the opposite side from where Megan was standing.

"Stay over there, please," Megan said and closed her eyes. Within seconds, she was back in her true form, a large slender dragon with ruby-red scales glimmering in the sunlight coming through the beams above. Her large grey wings were folded along her back. She took up more than half of the garden space, and her head was bent down so as not to hit the beams above.

"Megan! You're beautiful!" Lilya shouted. "I can't believe it. You were so small…" She stopped, realizing what had happened the last time she had seen Megan, the last time they were together.

"Yes, Lilya, I was much smaller when you last saw me," Megan replied, keeping strict control of her emotions, and focusing on the job at hand. "Jan, which wall is the front wall? If we can burn that one down, it would be better than trying to fly out."

Pointing to the front wall, Jan answered, "That is the one. We will stay here, and let you make a way out."

Positioning herself so that her flames would not bounce back onto Jan and Lilya, Megan started to blow fire toward the wall. However, as it burned, the smoke from the burning wall was filling the room, and Jan and Lilya started coughing.

"This will not work; we must fly out!" Megan quickly turned the flame onto the beams and burned them out, burning off the net along with them.

As soon as there was enough room to leave, Megan shouted to the others, "Quickly, get on my back. Jan, help Lilya with her tree. We must leave now as I hear them coming back!"

Jan helped Lilya up on Megan's back and got her positioned so the tree was between Lilya and Megan and would not fall off. Then Jan climbed on across from Lilya, to make sure they both held on tight. "Okay, Megan, we're ready! Go!"

Suddenly, there was a great commotion at the locked door, sounds of furniture being pulled away, and a key was hastily inserted and unlocked the door.

"Hang on!" Megan shouted. She took off just as the door flung open and the man ran into the room. She could hear him screaming to his family as they flew into the clouds above.

Once they had the cover of the clouds, Megan headed back to the forest where they met the deer yesterday, landing in an open field that was surrounded by trees.

It took a bit longer for Megan to transform back into a human this time. She felt much more secure as a dragon; however, she knew that being a human was the only safe form. After closing her eyes and focusing a minute or two, she had become a human again, at least in form.

"What now?" Lilya asked softly, looking at Megan, not sure of what would happen next.

"We need to complete our real mission," Megan replied and headed into the forest.

Chapter Eleven

BACK TO THE FOREST

Megan led the way with Jan and Lilya behind her. Megan's dragon senses would make it easy to get back to Bonnie and the deer that had been given medicine last night. Within a few minutes they were back, and what a different sight from what they walked into yesterday!

Megan and Jan smiled and waved to the deer as they entered the clearing. All the deer had recovered enough to sit up and were quietly eating the soft grasses that had been provided by their helpers.

"Hi Megan and Jan!" called Bonnie as she walked toward them. "I am happy to report that all ten of the deer are eating well and their health has greatly improved. Thank you so much for your help in their recovery!"

"That is good news, Bonnie," Megan replied. "I will be sure to let Ituria know that the medicine worked, and to thank him and Simon on your behalf. I'm glad that we were able to help."

"You have definitely helped us. Thank you. Is there anything we can do to stop our friends from getting sick?" Bonnie asked. "We don't want to have to go through this again."

Jan replied, "The only suggestion Ituria had was to not pick up anything from the ground, even if it smells like the treats that the humans are giving to them. Please let all the deer know this!"

Bonnie nodded, agreeing with the instructions. "I will let them know what Ituria has said. Hopefully, we can all learn from this. Humans have been feeding us for years, and sometimes the younger deer forget what they are supposed to be eating. They need to know that they should be eating the grass and leaves of the forest, and not only human food."

"I am so glad that the deer are feeling better, and I hope that this does not occur again. However, if it does, please let Ituria know, and we will bring more medicine down for your friends. We will leave you now and wish you well." Megan bowed to Bonnie and headed back to into the forest.

"Take care everyone!" Jan shouted as she waved goodbye, then turned to follow Megan with Lilya at her side.

Finding a clearing next to a large tree, Megan sat down and motioned for the others to sit with her. "We have had a very eventful few hours here on Earth, Jan, and have learned many things." She paused for a moment, then continued, "Lilya, we still have much to discuss, but most of those discussions must wait for another day. Our most immediate issue is that we have now stolen you from a local family, and if they have a dragon as they stated, they will be searching for you—and now for me also, since they have seen me in my dragon form."

"My plans would be to get Jan back to her research camp, then return to Ituria's Island. However, Lilya, I am not sure you would want to go there, or if you would be welcome." Megan's voice was calm, reciting their current situation and seeking a resolution; emotions could be dealt with later. "I have been told that you stole something from Ituria and came to Earth. This is different from what you told me so many years ago. Can you explain?" Megan stopped and looked at Lilya, waiting for her response.

Lilya eyes opened wide as she realized just how much Megan knew. She had been caught in her lies and knew she had to tell the truth, no matter what her fate.

"You are correct, Megan, and I did not tell you the truth before." Lilya's voice was soft and hesitant, not wanting to admit that she had lied to Megan. "I had been on Ituria's Island for a long time at the request of the Goddess Hesperides. One night, I was feeling lonely for Earth, and decided to sneak away. I didn't know what would happen if I asked to visit Earth, and so I just stole one of the golden apples and left." Lilya lowered her head as she recalled what she had done. "That was wrong, and I know that now." Lilya looked up at Megan and continued, "I would never have done it if I knew what the consequences would be. You must believe me!" Lilya's eyes filled with tears, waiting for some type of response from Megan.

"As I said, we will discuss that later." Megan would not allow her emotions to take control. "We must leave as soon as possible, and I would suggest going back to the research site and updating Mr. Russell; we can make further plans once we are away from this place. Do not underestimate the power of a dragon; if there is one looking for us, it will find us, even hidden in this forest!"

"I agree with your plan, Megan," Jan said, nodding her head. "We should not remain here. Let's leave now and make plans once we have reached the camp. Mr. Russell may also be able to help us with Lilya's situation." Jan stood and helped Lilya up, then handed her the potted tree, and they backed away from Megan. "Ready when you are!"

Without another word, Megan transformed back into a dragon and waited for Jan and Lilya to climb onto her back. Launching into the sky, she quickly sought the safety of the clouds that would block her from view as she headed back to camp. She didn't know what would happen there; she just knew they couldn't stay here any longer. The danger was too great.

Chapter Twelve

DANGER FOLLOWS

Peering through the clouds, Megan spotted the island where Mr. Russell's research camp was located and confirmed there were no researchers on Site 4 where she wanted to land. However, there was something large on Site 3, and she flew just a little closer to see what was going on; Mr. Russell indicated that Site 3 was off-limits. No one was allowed to go there. *Have the poachers returned?*

"Jan," she called back, wanting Jan to check it also. "See what is going on at Site 3 as we pass over it. It doesn't look right. Did the poachers come back?"

"I will look," Jan replied, opening her eyes. She wasn't used to flying on the back of a dragon and felt more comfortable closing her eyes and hanging on tight. As she looked at Site 3, she gasped and shouted, "It's a dragon in front of the cave!"

"I see it, too!" Megan called out. "Let's go to Site 4. We won't be visible from there." Swooping silently down to Site 4 and out of view from the dragon on Site 3, Megan gently landed. As soon as

Jan and Lilya were off her back, she transformed into a human. "From this distance, the dragon may not be able to smell me. However, we need to be very careful because if there is a dragon here, most likely he carried a human with him!"

"Agreed!" Jan exclaimed, planning how to proceed. Neither Megan nor Lilya could be spotted in camp. "Why don't we all go to my tent? Then you and Lilya can remain hidden there while I find Mr. Russell. Will that work?"

"Yes," Megan replied. "We will follow you; we must get hidden quickly in case the dragon saw us!"

"Lilya, since you are on natural ground, will you allow me to carry the tree?" Megan asked. "It will be much quicker if you don't have to balance the tree as we are going down this path."

"Yes, thank you, Megan. Since there is grass and other living plants around here that I can touch, I should be able to proceed without holding the tree." Lilya held out the pot for Megan to hold.

Jan looked down at her feet. "Megan, quick note—we both left our shoes back at the house, so we must be careful not to cut our feet on the sharp rocks as we go back to camp. Lilya, you will also have to watch out for any rocks that may damage your feet."

Staying on the grassy areas and away from the rocky path, the trio made it back to camp and quickly slipped into Jan's tent. "Stay here and keep quiet!" she whispered. Then she grabbed and put on a pair of sandals and headed out to search for Mr. Russell.

It didn't take long for Jan to find him. Angry voices could be heard from inside the supply tent; it was Mr. Russell arguing with someone else. Stopping outside to listen to the voices, she was able to identify the person arguing with him—*the homeowner*!

"What do you mean you have them trapped?" Mr. Russell asked in a loud voice.

"I have the girls; I will kill them unless you return the moon goddess!" was the response. Anger and frustration filled these words, and Jan knew exactly who it was—the homeowner must have flown by dragon. *But how did he know where to go?*

"What makes you think they stole anything? The girls are my researchers. They wouldn't steal! If you have them, you must return them immediately!" Mr. Russell was very angry and very concerned.

"Girls were very tricky—they lied to me. One turned into a dragon. Give me the moon goddess!"

"I am calling the authorities; you cannot kidnap my researchers!" Mr. Russell was yelling now.

Jan had to let Mr. Russell know they were okay and were not being held prisoners, even if that meant confronting the man who had trapped them earlier. Summoning all her courage, she opened the tent flap and walked inside. "Mr. Russell, we are not his prisoners. We are both here."

"Thank goodness!" Mr. Russell exclaimed. "I was so worried that this man really had trapped you. Are you okay?"

"We are safe. This man tried to trap us, but we escaped," Jan responded, letting Mr. Russell know that they were still in danger.

"No!" shouted the man as he started running toward her. "You are thieves! You must return the moon goddess now!"

Stepping in between Jan and the man, Mr. Russell shouted back, "No, you will not go near her! You are in serious trouble. I am going to have you arrested for threatening my researchers!"

"I will have my dragon kill you all!" he shouted, shaking his fist in the air.

"No, you won't! Not if I talk to him first!" Jan shouted and ran out of the tent.

The man started after Jan, but Mr. Russell grabbed his wrist. "You will leave her alone!"

Shaking off Mr. Russell's grip, he shouted, "No, I will not. My dragon will kill you all, and I will get back the moon goddess!"

Chapter Thirteen

The Story of Tsuyo and Shinju

Running to her tent, Jan quickly stuck her head inside and yelled, "Megan, come now! I need you! Lilya, stay hidden!" Then she started running up the path to Site 3, knowing Megan would be able to catch up. As she turned onto the path, she looked back and saw Megan running toward her; she also saw Mr. Russell and the homeowner leaving the supply tent. As soon as he saw her, the man started running toward her, and Mr. Russell followed. It was now a race to Site 3 and who could reach the dragon first!

Megan looked back at the men chasing them. As soon as she and Jan rounded a corner and could not be seen, she transformed into a dragon and flew up to Jan, picking her up by the shoulders and continuing up the path, asking, "Where are we going?"

"Site 3," Jan said, breathing hard. "The dragon belongs to the man who trapped us—he is going to order it to kill us! We need to get there first!"

"On our way!" Megan replied and headed for Site 3, making it in only a few minutes. She landed far enough away where they could not be seen by the dragon and transformed back into human form. "This will be better for us to approach the dragon, and it is better if I am in this form when the man and Mr. Russell make it to the site."

"Agreed!" Jan replied. "I have the translation stone, so we can both will speak to it, but please make sure I am talking and acting appropriately for dragon protocols!"

Looking back down the path, Jan could see Mr. Russell far below and shouted to him, "Mr. Russell, you must keep him from getting to the dragon!"

"Okay, let's go Megan!" Jan continued as they entered Site 3; there was not a moment to lose!

Lying in front of the cave entrance at the top of Site 3 was a large dragon, crimson red in color with ash-grey wings. It looked asleep; however, as soon as Jan and Megan entered Site 3, its ears perked up, its eyes opened and it stood up, sniffing the air. Taking a second long breath, it stared at the two humans approaching.

"Stand down, do not come closer, humans. This is my lair!" Jan was too far away for the translation stone to work, so she only heard loud growling and roaring, and stopped in her tracks. Megan understood and kept walking.

"Greetings fellow dragon. I am pleased to make your acquaintance. I am Megan." Megan gave a formal bow to the dragon, then took Jan by the hand and brought her forward. "This is my human friend, Jan. She means you no harm." Following Megan's example, Jan also bowed to the dragon.

"I am confused at how you smell and act like a dragon but appear to be human. Please explain. My name is Tsuyo, and I am pleased to make your acquaintance." Tsuyo then formally bowed to both Megan and Jan.

"Greetings, Tsuyo. I have taken a magic potion to allow me to take this form when I am with humans. How did you come to be here at this cave?" Megan was slowly getting closer to Tsuyo, and bringing Jan also, so that Jan would be able to follow the conversation. When they got within ten feet, Megan stopped and motioned for Jan to stop also.

"Tsuyo is a name I remember from many, many years ago. How did you come to be here?" Megan said, repeating her question, needing an answer. Memories from her time before Lilya were popping up in her head. *Where did Tsuyo fit in? I must remember!*

"My human captor has flown me here to find something that is lost. I must remain here and let no one enter the cave." Tsuyo dropped his head, ashamed to reveal that he was a captive of humans. "I am sorry, but I cannot allow you to enter the cave. Why are you here?"

"Tsuyo, do you remember when you were small? How did you become a captive of humans?" Images were appearing in Megan's head, when she was small there was another dragon, and they were captured together and then split up. *I was given to Lilya, who changed my name from Shinju to Megan and locked me in the cave, and this may be—my brother, Tsuyo!* Megan listened intently to see if her story matched his.

"When I was very young, my sister and I were captured by a samurai; in exchange for our lives, I was bound by an oath to the humans not to let the moon goddess leave with the bonsai tree, and my sister was given to the moon goddess. I have not seen her since then. I have been chained in a cave by my captors very close to their home, and each night I stand guard in front of the garden, keeping the moon goddess from leaving the garden."

"Then today," Tsuyo continued, very distressed, "I was told that I had allowed the moon goddess to escape and was flown here so that my human could recover her. He told me I would be punished for allowing her to escape, and my sister will be killed as part of my punishment." Tsuyo dropped his head in sadness. "I haven't seen her in so many years, and now they will kill her. I don't know what I can do to save her. If you would assist me in any way, I would be eternally grateful."

Memories were flooding back. Megan remembered Tsuyo as a small dragon, playing together with their mother. Then the image appeared she tried so hard to forget—humans came and brutally killed their mother, dragging the two young dragons away in chains. She had not seen Tsuyo since that terrible day.

"Tsuyo!" Megan cried out. "I am Shinju, your sister!"

Chapter Fourteen

No Going Back

Looking at Megan, Tsuyo's eyes grew wide—he got closer to her and took several deep breaths. "Is it really you? Where have you been? I have been told I can never leave or they will kill you—how did you escape?"

Before Megan had a chance to answer, the man ran onto Site 3 and started yelling at them as he got closer. Mr. Russell was not far behind but could not keep him away any longer.

"Tsuyo," Jan started quickly, trying to explain the situation to him, "you were bound by your dragon oath not to let the moon goddess leave with the bonsai. Know that she did leave, but she did not take the bonsai, so you have fulfilled your obligations under your oath and are no longer bound to these humans!"

"And they cannot use the threat of killing me to keep you in chains either, as they no longer control me," Megan added. "Jan rescued me from this cave just a few weeks ago. You are now free from all oaths.

Please, return with me to my new home where there are no humans to imprison you!"

The man was within ten feet now and could understand the conversation. "No! You belong to me; you can never leave!"

The full importance of what had happened was dawning on Tsuyo. He was now free—after so many years of cruel punishment and captivity by the humans. He stared at the tiny human running toward him. "How dare you claim me as your prize! I do not belong to you. I was only bound by my oath as I protected the life of my sister. I will never go back with you!"

"You do belong to me! You were given to me, so you are mine! You will obey me!" He was not backing down.

"You will not speak to me like that. I am your prisoner no longer. Your ancestors killed my mother. That does not mean that you own me... I am a dragon!"

Raising his head up high, Tsuyo flapped his wings in defiance. The wind generated by his wings knocked the man to the ground. Finally realizing that he no longer had control, the man started backing up, but his eyes were searching around for something, anything, that would give him back the advantage. What could he do?

Mr. Russell called out to Jan, "Jan, tell Megan the moon is visible. They can go now!"

Jan looked over to the east and could see the moon rise over the horizon, almost invisible in the daylight. "Megan, the moon. You and Tsuyo need to go, now!"

"Brother," Megan called to him, "come with me and start a new life on the moon where humans do not hunt and kill animals or dragons. It is run by Ituria, who has made it a haven for animals persecuted by evil men. Please, join me!"

"Should I not seek revenge for all of their evil? Is that not the right thing to do?" Tsuyo asked, his anger building. "They should be punished!"

"No! Do not become like them!" Megan pleaded. "Let us leave and enjoy together the freedom we have never had!"

"Sister Shinju," he replied. "For you, I will allow them to live. Please let us leave now before I change my mind!"

"Thank you, dear brother!" Megan said, instantly transforming into a dragon almost as large as her brother. Turning toward the moon, she shouted, "Guardian, look for the blue light!"

Flapping her large wings forward, a blue beam was created that encircled her and Tsuyo, pointing to the moon. As Tsuyo looked around, wondering what was happening, she shouted, "Guardian, now!" and both were drawn into the blue beam and disappeared, almost as if they had never been there.

Jan looked at the man as he got off the ground. At first, he was in awe of the spectacle he had just seen, but he was no longer scared and was ready to go on the attack again. "Now look what you have done! You have cost me my dragon! You will pay for this!"

"No, I think you have done more than enough here. You will leave now, or you will be arrested." Mr. Russell was done trying to reason with this man whose family had perpetuated the captivity of Megan, Lilya, and Tsuyo for so long.

"You stole my dragon—at least give me the moon goddess to keep my bonsai alive! You owe me that!"

"We owe you nothing!" Jan shouted back. "Your ancestors kidnapped Lilya, promised her a safe place to live, then locked her in your garden. There is no honor in what you or your ancestors did, and you are owed nothing!" Jan had seen enough of this man's arrogance, and she wasn't going to take it anymore.

"If you ask nicely, maybe Mr. Russell will allow you to be given a ride to the mainland; otherwise, you can swim back. It is time for you to leave!" Jan turned and walked away from the man and Mr. Russell, heading back to camp to check on Lilya.

Chapter Fifteen

Lilya's Side of the Story

As Jan headed back down from the cliffs, she could hear Mr. Russell talking with the man. They were walking behind her, arguing, and she decided that she would not go directly back to her tent as the homeowner would be watching her to see where Lilya might be. She went to the supply tent and grabbed some fruit and cheese, waiting for Mr. Russell and the man to walk by as they headed to the dock.

She overheard Mr. Russell say he would take the man back to the mainland, but he must never return, or he would be reported to the authorities. Once Jan heard the boat leave the dock, she headed back to her tent with the food. As she reached her tent, she entered quietly, and softly called to Lilya. "Lilya, I'm back."

She looked around the tent but didn't see her. *Where could she be?* "Lilya, where are you?" Jan asked softly. "You can come out now."

"Okay, Jan. Here I come," said a small voice from under Jan's bed. "You told me to hide, and this is the only place I could find."

Holding onto her tree as she emerged from under the bed, Lilya sat on the bed. "Is he really gone? Am I really free?"

"Yes, you are no longer trapped with the bonsai. You are free," Jan said calmly. "Where you go from here will be up to you. I wanted to let you know that you did have a role in freeing Megan."

"What?" Lilya exclaimed. "I was trapped. I could do nothing! What are you saying?"

"Do you remember a little statue in a silk bag that was left at the entrance to the cave?" Jan asked, wondering who would have put it there if she didn't.

"Yes, I remember," Lilya said slowly. "I never did trust the samurai; his words were too conflicting. His promises kept changing. I left the figure and a map in a vase, so that if Megan and I were trapped in the cave by the samurai, someone could find us."

"But I had figured it wrong," she continued. "He wasn't going to trap me in the cave, only Megan. Once he found I had special talents with plants, I had to remain with his bonsai plant to keep it alive. Should I ever think of trying to escape, he showed me a map of where the cave was, saying that his men would kill Megan if I left him."

"Generation after generation, they showed me the map, telling me that if I left the bonsai tree that they would kill Megan." She thought for a moment, then smiled as she continued. "One thing I did not tell them was that the apple tree grew magic apples. I told them I needed it to keep in touch with my own powers. I took care to eat all the apples before they ripened so that the samurai would not learn of their power."

"So, Megan was left there to use as a weapon against you? If you left, they would kill her?" Jan was amazed. There were many sides to the intertwined stories of Lilya, Megan, and Tsuyo!

"When I started to suspect he had evil plans, I made the map and hid it at the entrance to the cave. The little man you found was one of many carved warrior statues. The samurai had them made to demonstrate his wealth and power to others. Each represented one of his many warriors. He had so many statues—he did not miss one little man or the horse I hid in the roots of my other apple tree."

"I am so glad that finally my Megan was rescued. However, I fear that she will never forgive me for leaving her there. As sad as I am that she was trapped for so long, she must carry as much anger against me for being trapped there. The only thing I can hope for is that she and her brother will finally be able to spend some happy time together. I do not expect her to forgive me and only wish her peace." Lilya started slowly shaking her head back and forth. "I'm not sure if I would forgive me if I were her." Then she stopped talking, not sure what else she could say. She clutched her little apple tree to her, her only comfort during her own captivity, and closed her eyes.

"Why don't you take a rest on this bed?" Jan said. "I will stay with you to keep you safe."

"Yes, my dear Jan. I would like to sleep in a safe place. Thank you for your kind offer." Lilya turned and laid on the bed, holding her tree as close as she could, and closed her eyes. Jan sat down in the chair next to the desk, positioning herself so she could see both Lilya and the tent opening. As Megan said, it had been a very eventful day so far, and Jan hoped that it would be a very uneventful afternoon.

She knew she would have to stay awake, despite having no sleep last night, so she made a cup of tea in her little teapot and waited for Mr. Russell to get back to camp. She had many pages of notes on the new chicks to index and report, and she focused on updating the tallies.

Hearing something in the distance, she looked up and around the tent, trying to focus on the direction and the source of the noise. Now she could hear yelling in the distance, then the sound of running in between the several tents. It wasn't going to be a quiet afternoon after all!

Chapter Sixteen

UNEXPECTED VISITORS

"Lilya," Jan whispered as she touched her shoulder, "you need to hide now! Back under the bed—hurry!" Jan helped Lilya get under the bed, then she pulled the blanket over so that the space between the bed and the floor was covered. Lilya would not be visible if someone walked into the tent. Then Jan laid on top of the bed, pretending to be asleep, listening intently for what might happen next.

Since Knocker and her dad had gone, there were only three researchers at camp: Mr. Russell, Justin, and herself; there were also two residents hired to cook and keep the research camp clean, Jeff and Robert. Mr. Russell had taken the homeowner back to the mainland and would have had Jeff pilot the boat. That left Justin, a researcher who joined the camp shortly after Knocker went home, and Robert, who oversaw the kitchen and pantry.

Two local fishermen were hired to stay at the dock to keep out poachers, but they were always on their boat and never came into camp. *Who else is here?*

She could hear someone running through the camp and Jan was hoping they wouldn't come into her tent. Pretending to be asleep should anyone peek in; she kept an eye on the tent flap.

"Jan, where are you?" shouted Justin from the walkway between the tents. "Are you okay?"

Recognizing his voice, she replied, "Justin, I'm in here. What's going on?" Jan sat up on the bed but didn't move farther, wanting to keep herself between anyone coming into the tent and Lilya hiding under the bed.

As Justin opened the flap door, he explained, "Two men have just come into camp; they are looking for three girls who stole something from them. I told them we only had one girl on the research party, so they must be in the wrong place."

Walking into her tent, Justin added, "They didn't listen to me; they had a map of the island and started running up the cliff. Do you know anything about this?"

"No, I don't think so," Jan said quietly, trying to figure out what was happening. "Do you know when Mr. Russell will be back?" *Maybe these two men are family of the homeowner? They have a map of the island just like Lilya said!*

"He and Jeff left about an hour ago, so I would expect them to get back in the next half hour or so, as it takes just over an hour to get to the mainland

and back, and he had to drop off that guy—do you know what that was all about?"

"It was just some weird guy who started yelling at me on the cliff, and Mr. Russell escorted him off the island. I don't know how he got here. Maybe one of the locals dropped him off."

Walking closer to Jan, Justin said, "Mr. Russell told me to stay by the dock to make sure no one came on the island, but just now, these other two guys showed up." Justin sat in the chair next to the bed, slowly getting closer to Jan. "I will stay here with you. We'll need to wait until we have more back-up before we can continue."

"I agree. Do you know where Robert went? Is he still in camp?" Jan wanted to know where everyone was. "We'll need to let him know of the intruders as well."

"He might have been in the supply tent," Justin replied, looking like he was trying to remember something.

"Can you please go check? We need to make sure he's safe. I'll stay here. It's probably the safest place for me as I don't want to run into those men until Jeff and Mr. Russell get back."

"Yeah, sure. Just stay here, okay? It may not be safe running around outside," Justin said as he got up and went to the tent entrance. "I'll only be gone a few minutes."

"I'm not going anywhere. I promise!" Jan replied.

As soon as Justin left the tent, Jan leaned over the side of the bed and whispered to Lilya, "No matter what, do not come out. I am not telling anyone you are here. Do not speak—even to me." Sitting up quickly, she waited for Justin to return. It was just a minute later when he walked back into the tent.

"I checked on Robert. He's fine," Justin started. "He's getting ready to start prepping for lunch, said he was going to wait until Mr. Russell got back before cooking anything."

Justin sat back down in the chair and looked at Jan carefully. "You don't think this has anything to do with that Megan girl who was here, do you?"

"What do you mean?" Jan asked, wondering where this conversation was going. Justin wasn't here when Megan first came to came three weeks ago, and Megan was only on the island for a few hours last week. She stayed on Site 4, never came into camp. *Justin never met Megan!*

"Well, Robert said that before I got here there was a girl named Megan who stayed for one night, right when Knocker left," Justin replied. "This morning I was on Site 2, and I saw you and two other girls coming down the path to camp, and one of the girls was carrying something."

Jan tried to remain calm, but inside she was panicking. *We were seen coming back to camp!*

Justin leaned toward Jan as he continued. "So, there seems to be a good reason for why these men are here. You need to tell me what is going on now and where the other two girls went."

Chapter Seventeen

HEADING TO SITE 3

"**W**hat are you talking about?" Jan said, trying to keep her voice calm, realizing Justin was not here to keep her safe, but to keep her prisoner while the other two men searched for Megan and Lilya.

"Come on, Jan. Mr. Russell isn't here to protect you now." Justin stood up, looming over Jan as she sat on the bed. His voice got louder, more insistent. "I know there is something on Site 3, something valuable. That's why no one is allowed up there. Is that where the girls are hiding?"

"Look, I'm willing to deal with you," he continued in a calmer tone, cracking a fake smile. "That is probably not the case with the two men who came through earlier. Wouldn't you rather work with me?"

"Look, Justin," Jan replied, trying to reason with him, "I don't know what you're talking about. Someone has been filling your head with tall tales. Site 3 is where the poachers were stealing eggs. That's why it is off limits. One of them pulled a knife on me. That's why we have guards at the dock and why no one goes to Site 3."

"Don't use your little innocent stories on me. Robert told me lots of stuff, stuff he saw, stuff he heard." Justin's voice had revealed a menacing tone. He was here to find some fantastic treasure, and there was no way she would convince him otherwise.

"Look," Jan said, realizing she had to get Justin out of the tent, "let's go up to Site 3 and take a look around. Maybe that will convince you that there is nothing there worth stealing." Jan stood up and walked over to the desk, taking out a paper and pencil. "Let me write a note to Mr. Russell, then we will head up to Site 3. Okay?"

"Okay, but don't get cute in the note. No telling Mr. Russell what we are looking for—none of his business! Got it?" Justin was yelling at her now.

Justin stood close behind Jan, looking over her shoulder as she wrote the note. *What can I say? What will Mr. Russell understand?* She wrote a short note, knowing she couldn't say much, and hoping it would be enough.

Justin nodded with approval; it sounded okay to him.

Carefully placing the note in the middle of the desk, she started walking out of the tent. "Wait a second!" she said as she went toward the small closet. "Let me get my backpack. You never know when you might need something walking up the cliffs." Jan took a quick look inside —a flashlight, water, some notebooks, and pencils.

"Okay," Jan continued, trying to sound a little cheerful, "let me show you what is at Site 3, and that there is no treasure. That will put your mind at ease!"

"You're right, Jan. There probably isn't anything to this story, but I need to check it out, okay?" Justin said, attempting to be friendly as they started up the path. He was trying to get back on her good side. "I hope you aren't mad at me."

"No, no," Jan replied. "Let's answer your questions about Site 3, then we can go have some lunch with Mr. Russell." What she said to Justin and how she felt were entirely different, but if Justin wanted to play nice, it would make it easier to get up to Site 3.

She wanted to know how much Justin knew and what had Robert told him. *He saw us return, so he was dangerous at this point. What else does he know?* "So, what did Robert tell you? What stories has he been hearing around the campfires?"

"Well, not that I believe everything he said, you know. But he said there are legends about this island, treasure hidden in the caves. He also told me he saw you go up to Site 3 last night, and then you didn't come to dinner."

"I wasn't feeling that great, so I just took some bread and cheese from the supply tent and ate in my tent. That was all." Jan hoped she sounded sincere. There were a lot of things to keep track of to keep her story going. "And I did go up to Site 3. It's the best view on the island. In the mornings you can see the sunrise, and at night the sunset. It's very relaxing."

"That makes sense," Justin agreed. "But where did you go this morning and where did those other two girls go? I didn't tell the men I saw you, but I did see all of you walking down the cliff, and one of you was carrying something. I'm very curious." Justin tried to sound pleasant, but there was no mistaking his intent—he wanted the treasure. "Where did you go that I would see you coming down from the cliffs and what was one of you carrying?"

"We were at Site 4," Jan replied. "It's also a beautiful view. I had a late breakfast with my friends before they left, and one was carrying a pot with dishes and our food." Hopefully he would not dig further into why they were on the cliffs.

"Okay, but how did they leave?" Justin was getting more demanding, wanting to know what happened to them. "They didn't leave by the dock, so where did you leave them?"

"They left just before that man arrived. He was angry and yelling at everyone, so they just hid behind the boathouse until he passed, and then they got in their boat and left. Or at least that's what I would think. I went to my tent to take a nap and didn't actually see them leave the dock."

"Oh, you didn't see them leave!" Justin was grasping at every word she said. Maybe better not to say anything else. "So maybe they are still here! Maybe they went to Site 3 and are stealing the treasure!"

"Justin, for the last time, there is no treasure!" Jan exclaimed, hoping it would sink in.

"But I heard otherwise," he responded. "And I'm going to find out for myself!"

Chapter Eighteen

A Call into the Unknown

Walking faster and faster, Justin was in a hurry to make it up to Site 3. Jan wasn't in such a hurry, knowing there were two other men waiting there. If she slowed even a little, though, Justin would grab her by the elbow and push her along. "We are going to Site 3, so no trying to duck out on me, okay?"

"I'm not trying to duck out, it's just we are going up a steep path to the cliff, and I don't usually climb this quickly," Jan replied.

Looking around, she hoped to find some reason not to go up to Site 3. As she was searching, they came to the edge of one the cliff ledges, and she could see the moon over the eastern sea. *One chance in a million*, she thought, *but I'm going to take it.*

She had seen it happen twice before; both Megan and Knocker called out to Guardian, and he heard them! If there was a direct line from the Earth to the moon, they said, he was in range. Guardian knew her from her trip to Ituria's Island—*Maybe he will hear me. Maybe he can help!*

"Guardian!" Jan shouted to the moon. "Please find Megan!"

"What are you doing?" Justin screamed at her. "Are you trying to warn them? Not another sound out of you, you understand!"

Jan nodded slowly; she wouldn't say anything else. She knew that Justin wasn't going to let her go. If that didn't work, she would have to figure out another way to get away from Justin and the two other men.

She tugged on the straps to her backpack. With a flashlight, she could go into the cave on Site 3, and they wouldn't be able to follow. Even if they did try and follow, she knew the cave and could hide in one of numerous places where they couldn't see her. Okay, so that was at least a plan!

Looking down at her watch, it had been almost half an hour since they left camp. It took about forty-five minutes to get to Site 3, leaving her only fifteen minutes left to get away. Fifteen minutes before they met up with the two men looking for her, possibly the family of the homeowner who was here earlier today.

"Do you and the men have a bargain to share whatever you find?" Jan asked. *What relationship does he have with these men?*

"No! I don't think so!" Justin replied angrily. "I don't want to share with them or with Robert. Whatever I find is mine!"

"What kind of treasure did Robert say was here anyway?" Jan asked. "I was up here numerous times with my dad and never saw anything even remotely looking like a treasure chest or anything."

"He wouldn't tell me much. Maybe that's why he is here also, hunting for treasure!" Justin said begrudgingly. "He just said that this island had a legend of gold hidden in its caves and that's enough for me to take a look! Come on now. Walk faster!"

"But if you're not going to share, what are you going to tell those men when we get to Site 3? They may not want to share either!" Jan countered. Having Justin as an opponent alone was better than Justin and two other people. "And then there's Robert—is he going to demand a cut? Have you thought all of this out? What if you do find something? What then?" *Maybe I can convince Justin not to go to Site 3!*

"Not to worry!" Justin replied. "I can take care of myself!"

Pulling a small revolver out of his pocket and waving it in front of Jan, he grinned. "My dad said never leave home without it!" Then he carefully put it back in his pocket.

"Now, let's see what we can find on Site 3. It's just around this turn!" Grabbing Jan by the elbow once again, he hurried forward and stepped onto the flat portion of the cliff, looking around for the two men who had run up here earlier. "Do you think they may have gone somewhere else?"

"Look, up there!" Justin shouted. "I see the cave!"

Justin started running toward the cave entrance. *This could be my chance to get away!* As he put distance between himself and Jan, she backed up slowly. Mr. Russell should be back at camp now. As she was turning to run, Justin looked back. "What are you doing?" he screamed at her. "You said you would stay with me! Get back here!"

Jan took off running down the path toward camp as fast as she could, hoping she could run faster than Justin.

Chapter Nineteen

A Flash of Blue

As Jan was running, she thought she saw a flash of blue light in the direction of Site 4. *Did Guardian hear me earlier? Did he understand?* As the path to Site 4 came into view, she quickly veered off and headed that way. If she was wrong, she was trapped!

With Justin not far behind, she ran onto Site 4. She desperately looked around to see if anyone had responded to her call for help. *Yes!* Over near the rocks to the right, almost out of sight, she could see that Megan had returned!

She could hear running as Justin got closer. He was only a few seconds behind her. She ran over to Megan and whispered urgently. "Megan, we had breakfast on Site 4, you and Lilya left by boat, you took her home, you came back and were looking for me here, where I usually sit, okay?"

When Justin got within ten feet and the translation stone would work, Jan spoke in a louder voice. "Megan, I need your help! Justin has been told that there is treasure on this island, and he wants me to help him find it. Also, there may be two men on Site 3 who are connected to that mean guy who showed up this morning."

Justin stopped running when he realized there was someone else on Site 4 and was standing a few feet away. "Right, I asked Jan to help me go to Site 3. Isn't that right, Jan?" He tried to put a smile on his face, but it fell flat, and he stopped talking to catch his breath.

"Justin," Jan continued, also breathing hard from the run down the cliff. "This is Megan, a friend of mine. Megan, this is Justin." *Let's see what direction Justin plans on going from here.*

"Nice to meet you, Justin. How are you connected with this site?" Megan responded, looking carefully at Justin.

"Hi Megan. I came here a few days after someone named Knocker left. They needed another researcher. Nice to finally meet you!" Justin replied.

"Had you heard of me before? I don't remember seeing you." Megan turned to look at Jan, wondering what he was referring to, that he was glad to finally meet her.

"Justin saw you, Lilya, and I coming down from Site 4 after breakfast," Jan interjected into the conversation. "You were carrying a pot with our dishes, and he was wondering what we were doing up there." She had to make Megan aware of the story she told Justin.

"I told Justin that you and Lilya left," Jan continued, "but I'm glad you came back to join me during my research today on Site 4. Maybe we can show Justin that there really isn't any treasure on Site 3, but I'm still worried about the two men that ran up there earlier. We couldn't see them when we got to Site 3. Justin said they had a map of the island, so maybe they went into that cave."

Megan nodded; she was now aware of what was going on. *But one more thing she needs to know!* "Megan, you need to know that Justin has a gun!"

"Why did you say that?" Justin exclaimed, glaring at Jan. "Jan, I told you I had that gun so if we ran into trouble, I could protect you. I'll be able to protect you both if we run into those two guys. Two girls alone on the cliffs, you need protecting!" While Justin said he wanted to protect them, the look he gave Jan showed he was furious at her for revealing this to Megan.

"Jan, where is Mr. Russell? Shouldn't we get him involved in this situation?" Megan was trying to figure out why Justin was acting the way he was.

"Look, Mr. Russell left with that guy, and who knows when he will be back. I'm in charge while he's gone, so let's go back up to Site 3 and find out where those men went, okay?" Justin's tone was no longer friendly. He was going to Site 3, and they were going with him.

"Like Justin said, Mr. Russell went to the mainland to drop that guy off. Justin, you told me he would only be gone about an hour. Shouldn't we go back and see if he has returned?" Jan was hoping Justin might realize that Mr. Russell could be back at camp.

"Nope," Justin decided. "We are not going back to camp, we—all three of us—are going to Site 3 now. Got it?"

"Jan," replied Megan, in a calm voice, "we have been to Site 3 before. Let's go now and show Justin that there is no treasure." Megan walked over to Jan and put her arm around Jan's shoulder. "I'm here," she whispered. Then Megan and Jan started walking back up the path.

"I'm behind you now, so don't try anything funny like last time, okay?" Justin said as he started walking behind them.

Chapter Twenty

CONFRONTATION

As the trio walked onto Site 3, they could see two men standing near the cave. Both Jan and Megan looked at Justin, seeing what he would do next.

"Keep going!" he yelled at them.

The two men turned to see who was yelling and started walking toward them. Justin seemed nervous. Jan could see his hand slide into the pocket where he hid his gun, then he pulled his hand out again. *He's making sure it's still there.*

"What are you doing up here?" the first man asked as they got closer. "You need to leave!"

"I'm in charge of the research site while Mr. Russell is gone, so I need to know what you guys are doing." Justin stayed next to the girls, making sure they didn't run like Jan did last time. "What are you looking for?"

"None of your business!" he replied. "If you know what's good for you, you will leave and take these two girls with you."

Justin was taken aback, not sure what to do. He looked at Jan and Megan, then decided to try once more. "I heard there's a treasure up here; is that what you're looking for?"

"Where did you hear that?" the second man answered. "No, we're looking for our father. He said he would meet us here. Private family business, so you need to disappear, got it?"

"What is your father's name? Where does he live? And why would he want to meet you here, on an uninhabited island?" Megan realized these must be related to the man who had trapped her and Jan earlier this morning. "This area was provided for the exclusive use of Mr. Russell's research team. So please explain why you are here."

"Well, little lady," the first man replied. "Our father had some unfinished business here in that cave." As he spoke, he pointed to the cave at far side of Site 3. "He gave us this map and told us to meet him here as soon as we could."

Megan looked at Jan, nodding. "Okay, well he's not here now. He might be the one we saw being escorted off the property by Mr. Russell an hour or so ago."

"That's true," Justin added, trying to convince everyone, including himself, he was in charge. "Mr. Russell said this guy appeared and needed to be escorted off the property, and then he and Jeff took him to the boat and headed to the mainland."

"There you go!" Megan continued; she was not intimidated by these men. "If you are to meet your father, he has been here and is already gone. If we go back to camp, Mr. Russell should be back and can tell us where he dropped your father off."

"No, wait a minute," Justin said. "I still want to know what kind of treasure these guys are looking for. I deserve a share of it too!"

Megan glared at Justin and Jan shook her head; that was not the right thing to say.

"We're not looking for treasure!" the first man exclaimed.

"Then why are you here?" Justin was getting frustrated. "If there's no treasure, you need to leave now!"

"If we go back to camp, Justin, we can have Mr. Russell call the authorities." Jan was pleading with him. "We can let them discuss with these men why they are here, okay? Do you remember what I said about the poachers?"

"These guys aren't here to steal eggs!" Justin yelled and kicked several nests near him. "That's not why they are here. Are you?" He glared at the two strangers, trying to figure out why they would be here.

Jan gasped and ran to the broken nests, trying to put them back together, hoping the chicks were not hurt.

"I think we need to reconvene this discussion down in Mr. Russell's office." Megan's voice was calm but stern, and her meaning was crystal clear. She looked at the two men and Justin. It might seem like just a request to them, but Jan knew that Megan wasn't going to back down. No one was going to remain here on Site 3.

"No!" Justin yelled. "They need to tell me what is here, and why are they here!"

"No, they do not!" Megan retorted. "You need to represent Mr. Russell and do what he would expect you to do!" Megan's defiant stare at Justin silenced any further outbursts from him.

"And you two—you need to explain yourself to Mr. Russell, and if you have good cause to be here, he will let you return." Megan's voice was getting louder. She was done arguing with these tiny humans.

"Megan," Jan said softly, "let's head back to camp now, okay?"

"You'll go only when we say you can go. Got it, little girl?" The first man wasn't going to listen to some kid, and he put his hand on Jan's shoulder.

"Enough!" Megan yelled and instantly grabbed the man's hand, flipped him, and threw him hard to the ground. "You will not touch my friend!" The men stared at Megan in shock, their eyes wide and mouths open, not knowing how to respond.

"Megan, remain calm!" Jan called to her. "Let's just leave!"

"You are right, Jan," Megan replied, in a somewhat calmer voice. "Gentlemen, Site 3 is off limits. We will await you back at camp!"

Chapter Twenty-One

BACK AT CAMP

Heading straight for the path and not looking back, Megan took Jan's arm in hers, and they started walking down to the camp. There was a hushed silence behind them; the three men just stared, watching them walk away. No one even attempted to stop them.

Then Justin and the two men started arguing again, but Jan and Megan were too far away to understand. They were not following; however, at this point it didn't matter. At least Megan and Jan were no longer trapped on Site 3.

"Megan," Jan started, "thank you so much for returning. I called out to Guardian on the off chance he might hear me. Did he send you back?"

"Yes, he let us know you called to him," Megan whispered back, afraid her dragon voice might echo in the rocks. "I was meeting with Ituria about Lilya's fate when he called."

"Lilya!" Jan exclaimed. "She is still hidden. We need to hurry. She must be panicked by now. I had to get Justin out of my tent. That's why I agreed to come up to Site 3 initially. I couldn't let him find her."

Walking faster, they both felt the urgency to make sure Lilya was still safe.

"I do need to tell you one thing. Whether it will change how you feel about her is your own choice," Jan said softly. "Lilya said that she was told if she ever left, that they would come to the cave and kill you, Megan."

"What?" Megan asked. "Why didn't she say that to me this morning?"

"These men with the map, they must be looking for her—or for you," Jan continued. "Lilya said that each generation would show her the map and tell her if she ever left that they would come here and kill you. Now we know that this was not an idle threat; Lilya left this morning and there are already people ready to go into the cave."

Jan and Megan walked in silence, Jan letting Megan decide how to react to the news. They walked at a fast pace and were down back to camp in less than half an hour.

"Let's listen to see who may still be in camp," Megan whispered, then paused to listen before entering the group of tents. They could hear some pans and cooking noises at the far end of camp.

"Justin said that Robert was still here. He would be in the kitchen preparing lunch," Jan said quietly.

"Anyone else?" Megan whispered.

"No, not until Mr. Russell and Jeff get back," Jan replied.

"Okay, it seems clear for now," Megan said. "Let's go get Lilya."

"This way," Jan said quietly as she headed for her tent. As she walked in, she looked around, seeing if anything was different. The bed was the same. The note on the desk had moved. Someone had been in here!

"Lilya," Jan whispered in panic, "are you still here?" Jan went over to the bed and knelt beside it, peeking under the blanket where she had left her.

"Jan, you are back. Is it safe to talk?" Lilya was shaking with fear. "You said not even to answer you, remember?"

"You are safe now. Please come out. Megan has returned to protect us!" Jan said as she helped her get out from under the bed. "Who came into the room? Did they say anything?"

"Well, there were two men. They came into the room. One walked over to look at the desk and looked at your note," Lilya said. "I don't know who he was. As he ran out, he said something to the other, but I couldn't understand it."

"It must have been Mr. Russell and Jeff. It wouldn't have been Knocker because Lilya would have understood him," Megan said, thinking out loud as she sorted what could have happened. "Knocker did not come in, or he would have sensed Lilya was here."

Jan remembered that Knocker's keen sense of smell revealed everything in an area, whether he could see it or not. "Wait … when did Knocker get here?" Jan asked, totally confused now.

"He came the same time I did. He headed to camp, and I came to find you," Megan said calmly. "If they aren't here, I'm not sure where they might be now. We didn't pass them on the path to Site 3."

"We need to keep Lilya hidden. I'm sorry Lilya. We think the two men on Site 3 are the sons of the man who trapped us." Jan walked over and put her arm around Lilya's shoulder. "You will need to hide a little longer. We can't let them find you!"

"Jan, there's another option. I can see the moon from Site 4. Let's take Lilya there, and I can take her to Ituria's Island," Megan said. "Lilya, Ituria said you could come back if you vowed never to steal anything from him again. He has no problem with you visiting Earth if you are lonely. Also, Nya, another Forest Nymph, said she would make sure you had what you needed and weren't so lonesome."

"Really?" Lilya exclaimed. "That sounds so wonderful! I don't ever want to come to Earth again, *ever*! Yes, I agree. Thank you for taking my plea to Ituria, Megan! I cannot ask you to forgive me for all you have suffered because of me, but know that I am so glad you are now free!"

"Lilya, we have a lot to discuss, and I am glad you will come back with me to the moon." Megan reached out and took Lilya's hand in hers. "Now, let's get to Site 4 before anyone finds you!"

Chapter Twenty-Two

LILYA'S JOURNEY HOME

Megan went first, listening for anyone in the area, then waved for Jan and Lilya to follow. Lilya was carrying her tree, and they went as quickly as they could. It took about twenty minutes to get to Site 4; as they got close to the turn, Megan motioned for them to stay back and hide behind some large boulders.

"Jan," Megan whispered, "I hear some humans talking. I'm not sure if it is on Site 4 or coming down the path from Site 3. I cannot understand humans without you and the translation stone."

"Got it," Jan whispered back. "What should we do? We can't leave Lilya here."

"Let's go toward Site 4. If there is someone there, we will know very soon. But I'm thinking it's the humans up on Site 3," Megan continued. "We have to be prepared for anything. If I get the chance, I can call Guardian and get Lilya to the moon, and then come back to help you. There are some rocks on Site 4 where you can hide while I'm gone."

"Agreed," Jan replied as she started toward the turn to Site 4. "Get Lilya out of here!"

As she entered the turn, she heard the voices too, and she heard the angry dog sounds—that meant Knocker was there! But the sounds were not coming from Site 4. They were echoing from higher up. He must be on Site 3 arguing with Justin and the others. She pointed up the path to Site 3 and Megan nodded.

"Quickly," Jan murmured, waving Megan and Lilya towards Site 4. "You must hurry!"

"Lilya," Megan softly called, "I'm going to carry you until we get far enough to see the moon on the horizon—hold onto your tree!"

Gently lifting Lilya up, Megan started running toward Site 4, Jan following closely behind. Even though Megan was human in size, her dragon strength allowed her to reach the entrance to Site 4 in just a few minutes. She slowed to peek around the rocks and shook her head to Jan. There was no one there. They were safe on Site 4. Then she ran onto the site with Lilya.

Megan needed a direct line with the moon, which could be seen from only certain portions of Site 4. Once the moon was lined up, she set Lilya back on the ground.

"Lilya, you must stay still," Megan said softly. "I need to transform and form a blue beam of light so Guardian can find me, okay?"

"I'm just so scared right now… I will not move." Lilya's voice was breaking as she feared that she would be captured again. "Please, let us leave this place!"

"I'll stand at the entrance and let you know if anyone comes onto the site. Go, Megan!" Jan called to Megan, then ran back to the opening.

Megan stepped back a few feet, instantly transformed into a dragon, and waved her large wings toward Lilya. A blue beam of light encircled them both.

Jan could hear Megan calling to Guardian, but she was too far away to understand and only heard her dragon voice. Jan turned to look and saw Megan and Lilya disappear into the sky, no trace left behind.

Now there were footsteps running down the path from Site 3. Someone had seen or heard them. Jan ran behind one of the large boulders lining the far end of the site, hoping Megan would return soon.

Running footsteps got louder and closer, and Jan huddled deeper behind the rocks. Someone was entering Site 4! She could not be seen from the entrance, but she also could not see who was there. Whoever it was stopped and called out, "Hey, anyone here?"

Trying to figure out if she recognized the voice, Jan listened carefully. They shouted again, "Anyone here?" But the words bounced off the stone, making the voice hard to identify.

Could it be Justin? Could it be Mr. Russell? She couldn't tell! Better to stay hidden until she was sure it was safe.

At this point, Jan was frightened of everyone on the island. She was not going anywhere until either Megan, Knocker, or Mr. Russell found her. She could not trust anyone else at this point.

After a minute or so she heard footsteps leaving through the entrance, but she wasn't going to move yet. It could be a trick. A few minutes later, she could hear footsteps again—someone was still there! Jan sat huddled behind the rocks, wondering how long it took to travel to the moon and back to Earth. How long until Megan returned?

Chapter Twenty-Three

MEGAN RETURNS

Hiding being the rocks, Jan waited quietly. The footsteps she heard walked around the site, looking for something, stopping and starting again, but not coming her way. After several minutes, she heard the footsteps heading away, going back up the path to Site 3.

A few seconds after she could no longer hear footsteps, a blue light flashed in the opening. *Megan!* Jan stayed hidden, waiting for Megan to call for her. The soft growl she heard was Megan calling in her dragon voice! Slowly, she peeked around the boulder. She had to be sure before responding.

Megan was walking toward the boulders in her human form. As she got closer, her dragon voice changed. "…and we got Lilya back safe. I'm back and you can come out now!"

Jan ran out from behind the rocks, her courage renewed with Megan's presence. "I'm so glad to see you! There were some people here a few minutes ago.

I stayed hidden behind the boulders like you said and they didn't find me."

"Yes, I could see them from Guardian's viewing room," Megan replied. "I waited until they were gone before returning."

"I didn't recognize the voices. They echoed around the boulders," Jan added. "However, when I heard the voices from Site 3, I heard Knocker at one point in the conversation. He may be there. Should we go check?"

"Yes," Megan replied. "He may need reinforcements. If the two strangers are here to kill a dragon, then Knocker will not be able to transform." Then she sighed and said, "And then there's Justin!"

Walking quickly up to Site 3, they stopped just before the entrance; they could hear what was going on but could not be seen.

Jan could understand some of the conversation, and Megan other parts, as Knocker was having an animated conversation with the two strangers. Megan motioned for Jan to follow her as they headed back into the fray!

"Hi guys!" Megan called out as she got close enough for Jan's translation stone to work. "I waited for you down at camp, but you didn't show up. I've come all the way back, so I hope you have a good story as to why you should be here!" Her voice conveyed that she was not in the least bit afraid of them and maybe they should be afraid of her.

"Knocker, I see you have found our unexpected guests," Megan said as she got closer to him. "Have they shared anything with you?" Megan looked around, trying to determine where Justin went, and if anyone else was here. "Where did Justin go?" she asked Knocker, knowing the others wouldn't be cooperative.

Looking at Megan, Knocker answered a little cryptically. "I was told Justin said he was searching for treasure and decided to check out Site 4. I was also looking for Mr. Russell and Jeff, and these guys said they showed up and then left looking for Justin."

"Isn't that what you said?" Knocker asked them. "You saw two additional men come to Site 3 and then they left again?"

Both men looked at the cave, then at each other. Neither said anything. They weren't giving out any information.

"I think Jan and I will check out the cave, just to make sure Justin didn't run in there," Megan said after thinking about Knocker's message. "Jan, come on. Let's check out this cave everyone is so excited about." Nodding to Jan as she took her hand, she started walking away from the men and toward the cave.

"You can't go in there!" shouted the first man before she could take even a few steps.

"Why not?" Megan shouted back, turning so that Jan was behind her.

"What's in there belongs to me and my family! It's ours and we're going to take it!"

"What are you going to take?" Megan argued, her voice rising in volume. "What can be in that dark cave that you want? You will tell me now or I'm going to find out for myself!"

"Well, I think we should all take a look inside, don't you Megan?" Knocker added, going to stand next to Megan. They were both standing in front of Jan now, and she got the feeling that there was going to be a clash of wills and the dragons didn't want Jan to get caught in the middle.

"Jan," Knocker called back to her, still looking at the two strangers. "I see you have your backpack on. Do you still have your flashlight?"

"Yes, Knocker. I've got it," Jan replied.

"Why don't you take a look into the cave? Don't go too far back, though. Just see what might be behind the first row of rocks, okay?"

"Will do!" Jan called out as she turned and started running toward the cave.

"No!" shouted the second man. "There's nothing in there for you to see!"

"We will let her check it out for herself, okay?" Knocker said calmly. He and Megan stood solidly in front of the men, ready for whatever came next.

Chapter Twenty-Four

FINDING MR. RUSSELL

The two men looked at each other, then at Megan and Knocker. Judging by their last encounter with Megan, they were not sure about taking them on directly. Spreading apart about ten feet, the first man watched Jan as she entered the cave. His eyes got wide. He didn't want her going in and kept moving sideways while the second man watched Megan and Knocker.

"Megan," Knocker said, "why don't you make sure he doesn't interfere with Jan's inspection? I'll keep an eye on this one."

"Understood," Megan replied.

Megan walked in front of the first man, again blocking him from watching Jan. No longer close enough for Knocker's translation stone, she couldn't speak out for fear they would hear her dragon voice. But she didn't need to say anything; her cold stare told him that it would not be a good decision to try and get past her.

Knocker was having the same experience with the second man as he kept trying to maneuver past to get to the cave.

"Megan and Knocker," Jan called, not sure if they would understand or not, "all three are in here tied up and gagged. Be careful!"

The two men understood Jan's warning and tried to get around to the cave to capture her, too. But Megan and Knocker had other plans for them. Simultaneously, Megan and Knocker jumped into action. They reached out and threw the two men to the ground, pulling their hands behind their backs before they could even think of fighting back.

Megan grabbed the man's hands and pulled him back off the ground into a standing position, tightly holding him while Knocker dragged the other man to his feet. Niceties were over; there was no way these men would be able to break their grips. "I guess you guys don't really know how to tell the truth, do you?" Knocker said. "Let's go check out what Jan found in the cave, okay?"

By the time Megan and Knocker got there with their prisoners, Jan was able to free Mr. Russell and Jeff. She looked at Justin and hesitated. He wasn't really on their side, was he?

"Justin, please stand up," Jan ordered.

Still gagged and tied up, he struggled to stand up, and she reached over to help him. As he stood up, however, she quickly reached into his right pocket and took the revolver, putting it into her own pocket. "At least I don't have to worry about that anymore!" she said to him.

Then she backed up from him. "What got into you today? I'm not ready for you to be untied or ungagged yet, not until I talk with Mr. Russell. Understand?" Jan glared at him, and his eyes widened. He knew he had done something wrong, and it was the time of reckoning with Jan and Mr. Russell.

"Jan," Mr. Russell called out, "I'm so glad you are safe! Your note had me so worried, and I can see now why. I agree we will leave Justin tied up."

"Jeff, help me use these ropes to tie up these two men. Make sure they don't have any weapons after we get them securely tied," Mr. Russell continued. "Knocker and Megan, thank you once again for coming to rescue us. We are in your debt."

Turning his attention to the two men, he and Jeff tied them up securely, then gagged them. Getting everyone outside the cave, Knocker said, "I think it's time we all headed back to camp now. What do you think Mr. Russell?"

"Agreed," he responded. "We will have the authorities come take these two men off the island and possibly Justin also. I'm not sure what happened, but the note Jan left me said you were threatening her, and I don't take kindly to anyone threatening my friends."

Justin got a puzzled look on his face. What did he miss in the note? It looked fine to him.

"Don't look so confused, Justin," Jan said to him. "Mr. Russell just knows me a lot better than you do. Something you should have thought of before deciding that finding some unknown hidden treasure was worth your job and reputation. You will not be threatening Megan or me again!"

"Jan, when did Justin meet Megan?" Mr. Russell asked.

"He didn't meet her until late this morning, Mr. Russell," Jan explained. "He had heard she was here from Robert, who also told him tall tales about hidden treasures on Site 3. I tried to tell him it was off limits because of the poachers, but he wouldn't hear of it. He was determined to find a treasure, no matter what the cost." Jan was getting angry again and decided to herself that they needed to get back to camp and get everything sorted out.

Mr. Russell walked over to Jan and wrapped his arm around her shoulders. "If I knew that Justin would try something so stupid, I would never have left you alone, Jan. I'm just glad your friends, Megan and Knocker, were able to return to help out."

Leading the two men, Knocker started down the path to camp, and Megan grabbed Justin and led him down after Knocker. Jan and Mr. Russell followed behind. It was a quiet walk down. Three of the people were gagged, and the other four had had enough excitement for one day and were enjoying the quiet!

As she walked down next to Mr. Russell, Jan thought to herself that just twenty-four hours ago, she was happily counting little baby terns. Since then, she flew on a dragon, nursed some deer back to health, rescued Lilya, and got her back to the moon. What an adventure!

Chapter Twenty-Five

TYING UP LOOSE ENDS

As they got closer to camp, Mr. Russell looked at Jan and said, "Jan, you look exhausted! Why don't you grab a bite to eat and take a quick nap while Knocker, Megan, and I turn over these men to the authorities?"

"I think you read my mind, Mr. Russell!" Jan replied. The adrenaline that kept her going for the past twenty-four hours was wearing off, and the lack of sleep was catching up with her. Now that everyone was safe again, she was feeling very tired. "Megan and Knocker, please don't leave without saying goodbye, okay?"

"We won't, Jan," Megan responded quietly. "You've had quite a busy day, and you should know I couldn't have completed both missions without you!"

"I'll just take a quick nap, and then we can all have a late lunch together, okay?" Jan called to them as they dropped her off at her tent. Megan took a moment to check her tent out, just to make sure there was nothing surprising waiting inside. "Looks and smells clear!" she called to Jan. "I'll be back in a few minutes to check on you; just let me help Knocker for a moment."

Jan laid down in her bed and fell quickly into a deep sleep. She awoke to Megan gently shaking her shoulder. "Jan, why don't you join us for a meal before Knocker and I leave for home?"

"Oh, okay," Jan said sleepily. Sitting up, she rubbed her eyes, trying to remember everything that happened. "Did Lilya make it back okay?"

"Yes, Jan," Megan answered. "She will be able to start a new life there, and I told her that she and I would always be friends, that the past is behind us, and freedom is waiting for us on Ituria's Island."

Smiling at Megan, Jan was glad she had found it in her heart to forgive Lilya. Jan remembered Megan's brother, Tsuyo, was rescued also. "How is your brother? Does he have a place to call home up there?"

A great smile spread across Megan's face and her eyes sparkled as she remembered her brother. "Yes, he will stay with me. We will live on Ituria's Asian Coast Island and help the new residents. It is so good to have him back with me."

"One thing, Jan," Megan said. "Both of the men that were trespassing on the island were turned over to the authorities. However, Justin was just asked to leave the camp and taken to the mainland. Mr. Russell and I agreed that you are in danger and need to leave camp also, and he has asked that I fly you to your home. I told him I would be glad to do so."

Looking at Megan, she asked, "Why do I have to leave?"

"There is too much danger here for you now. Mr. Russell will be closing the research camp down in a week or so, once all the chicks have hatched. He fears that other family members may try to get onto the island, and he doesn't want to risk them finding you."

Sitting on the bed next to Jan, Megan continued, "Also, you and I know that there is no treasure buried in that cave, but the locals think otherwise. So, let's go have some lunch with Knocker and Mr. Russell, and then we can be on our way! One more flight on a dragon's back—are you up to it?"

"I am!" Jan exclaimed. "It was so exciting to soar through the air on your back! The first time it was scary, but then I realized how well you fly, how gracefully, and I'm looking forward to it!"

Walking into the dining area, Jan looked at Knocker and Mr. Russell talking together. She didn't want to leave, but she knew it was the best thing to do. She and Megan joined them at the table for some cheese and fruit.

"Mr. Russell, Megan has explained that I must leave. I understand why, but I hope you will include me on some of your other research projects." She glanced over at Robert in the kitchen, knowing she couldn't say anything else.

"Of course, Jan," replied Mr. Russell. "Knocker and I were just talking of some other projects that we needed to set up. I have your father's contact information and will definitely have you join us on other expeditions."

"Jan, you have been a true friend and ally, and we appreciate all the help you have given us. And I'm sure the little terns appreciate your help too!" Knocker said, smiling. "I look forward to working with you again."

After a quick lunch, Jan and Megan headed out of the tent. Jan packed up her clothes and items into her backpack and a small suitcase, and she and Megan headed back to Site 4 for the last time.

"Mr. Russell gave me a map of where to fly you, and it will only take a few hours," Megan said as they reached Site 4. "We will have to fly in the clouds, though, and I will need to get the translation stone back."

"I understand, Megan," Jan said as she slowly took the stone out of her pocket and put in Megan's hand. "I hope I'll see you again at some point. I know you have a new life on the moon so that may not happen." Jan's voice was sad, but she was trying to be cheerful. "I wish you and your brother all the best. You are finally free to be a family again!"

Megan looked at Jan as her face broke into a big smile. "Jan, my good friend, I'm sure we'll be seeing each other again. You can count on it!"

Jan smiled back, already looking forward to their next adventure!

THE END—until next time!

Note From The Author:

Although this is a fantasy fiction story, the truth is that plastic is hurting and killing wildlife, both on land and in the sea, and this harm is increasing every year.

One incident reported was that eleven wild deer at a deer conservation park died in 2019 because they ate the plastic wrappers left behind by human tourists. The humans threw the empty wrappers and bags on the ground rather than taking them back out of the conservation park, not realizing the danger the empty wrappers posed to the deer, who smelled the food odors and ate them. With their stomachs full of plastic, no real food could get through to nourish the deer. Once the cause of these deaths was discovered, additional steps were taken to educate the visitors, and it is hoped that these tragic deaths will not occur again.

Unfortunately, there is no magic pill that can cure the illness, pain and death caused by eating plastic. And there is no way of knowing what wild creatures have eaten plastic wrappers until after they have died. We must remember that there is a place for everything, and empty wrappers should not be left in the forest - or anyplace that wild creatures can reach them! They should be properly disposed of and recycled if possible. Reducing the use of plastics, and making sure to recycle what we do use, are some of the best ways to help Earth and its natural creatures.

Remember to reduce – reuse – recycle!

ABOUT THE AUTHOR

J.B. moved to Florida in her early teens and has lived there ever since, enjoying the mild weather and abundance of wildlife. She even spent several seasons raising orphan squirrels. She graduated from the University of Central Florida and has spent her working career in the legal profession. Her novels are inspired by her family and nature, as well as her need to escape from the real world once in a while.

www.facebook.com/J.B.Moonstar

Instagram @J.B.Moonstar

Twitter @jb_moonstar

jbmoonstar.author@gmail.com

website – jbmoonstar.com

BOOK CLUB QUESTIONS

1. Many birds are born with different colored
   feathers than their parents, (terns have tan
   feathers when born) and as they get their
   adult feathers, the feather colors match their
   parents (adult terns are mostly white). What
   benefit would baby birds living on the top
   of a cliff have in being a different color than
   their parents, such a tan?

2. Why did the note Jan receive have only drawings and no words or writing?

3. What marking did Jan find on both her little
   figure and the figure found by Megan?

4. Why is discarding plastic wrappers on the
   ground in the forest dangerous for wildlife?

5. How were Jan and Megan able to help the
   deer who had fallen ill after eating plastic
   wrappers from human food?

6. What is a bonsai tree and how is it different from other trees?

7. Why could Lilya not leave the bonsai garden?

8. Why can you see the moon during the day sometimes and only at night other times?

9. What was Justin seeking up on site 3?

10. Something to think about! Many wilderness hikers have a saying: "Take nothing but photographs – leave nothing but footprints." What do you think that means? What do humans leave when hiking or camping that could be dangerous for wild animals?

DISCOVER MORE BY JB MOONSTAR

CHRONICLES OF ITURIA

Russ and The Hidden Voice

Taylor and the Red Wolf Rescue

Jenna and the Legend of the White Wolf

Jenna and the Eyes of Fire

Jan and the Secret Cave

Jan and the Search for Lilya

Taylor and the Final Nine

Michelle and the Missing Manatee

Jenna and the Broken Promise

Sara and the Secret Mission

& More Adventures to Come!

THE MERMAIDS OF CRYSTAL CAY

Kimmi and the Sea Dragon

Roselia and the Ancient Warriors

& More Adventures to Come!

COLORING BOOK FROM

ARTIST JENN KOTICK

Mermaids

Discover more at
4HorsemenPublications.com

10% off using HORSEMEN10

www.ingramcontent.com/pod-product-compliance
Lightning Source LLC
Chambersburg PA
CBHW050419110726
47899CB00008B/2771